Joseph E. A. Smith

Souvenir Verse and Story

Memorial of fifty years

Joseph E. A. Smith

Souvenir Verse and Story
Memorial of fifty years

ISBN/EAN: 9783744747738

Printed in Europe, USA, Canada, Australia, Japan

Cover: Foto ©Andreas Hilbeck / pixelio.de

More available books at **www.hansebooks.com**

PITTSFIELD PARK, WITH THE OLD ELM, 1861.

SOUVENIR
VERSE AND STORY

MEMORIAL OF FIFTY YEARS

— BY —

J. E. A. SMITH

Author of Taghconic, The Poet Among the Hills, The History
of Pittsfield, The Genesis of Paper-Making, Etc.

"Like flakes of feathered snow,
They melted as they fell."
—*Dryden.*

SPRINGFIELD, MASS.
CLARK W. BRYAN COMPANY, PUBLISHERS,
1896.

We are growing old—How the thought will rise
   When a glance is backward cast
Of some long remembered spot that lies
   In the silence of the past:
It may be the shrine of our early vows
   On the tomb of our early tears;
But it seems like a far-off isle to us
   In the stormy sea of years.

— Frances Browne.

CONTENTS.

EXPLANATORY PROLOGUE.

This little volume, although for the most part rhythmic in form, is no ambitious attempt to claim for the author either the art or the inspiration of a poet. It is simply a collection of verses written during the last fifty years, and most of them published in one way or another. To these are attached some scraps of prose which may add to their value as mementos of the past, or as connected with interesting localities. Many of the verses were elicited by circumstances or occasions of which they have now become souvenirs for the writer and others. In the course of a long life of prose writing and editorial work, there has come to him now and then, although not often, a thought or a story which it seemed could be better treated in verse, and he so treated it. The lyrical pieces are selected from a multitude written chiefly to the order of musical publishers or composers, and which, having served their temporary purpose, have for the most part been forgotten. The children's songs are inserted simply to gratify the writer's love for the little ones.

He trusts that his readers share that affection.   If
they do not, he has no hope of their indulgence for
himself.   The translations speak for themselves.
Some of them are as literal as I could make them
consistently with English versification : but there
are several of which I have not the German originals
at hand, and I cannot recollect whether the translations are free or literal.   All the verses in the book
have either acquired a souvenir character from time,
or, as in the one piece just written, obtain it from
their themes ; and it is primarily in that role that I
here present them. Of course, however, I should not
offer them a second time to the public in any role,
if I thought them entirely devoid of merit.   It would
be an absurd affectation of modesty to pretend it.
Many of these verses, on their first publication, were
received with generous favor by my editorial breth-
ren of the old newspaper press, and by other perhaps
equally partial critics ; and I may be permitted to
hope that they may yet give a little pleasure to some
new readers.   Still it is primarily as mementos of
the past that they are now collected.

These last few words mournfully remind me how
few remain of those who would have looked kindly
on.these pages " for the sake of auld lang syne."
But I will not bore you with prosing regrets that

what is past is past, nor with the vain plaints of threescore-years-and-ten, over the universal and inevitable. " That which is without all remedy should be without all regard." Wise men wisely prefer Chronicles and Revelation to Lamentations.

It is better to present even a shadowy picture of the pleasant times that have been. Although most of those, to whom this picture would have recalled the memory of the pleasant things enjoyed by themselves have passed to a life of higher and fadeless happiness, their children may welcome some of these verses for their sake, and many of the younger generation may prize them as mementos of occurrences made familiar to them by history or tradition, or as connected with natural scenery which is as beautiful for them as it was for those who viewed it with me in the long ago; and for whose loveliness and grandeur my eyes are still undimmed.

And again : so intrinsically like is one human life to another that what is directly a souvenir for one heart may by association of ideas become incidentally so for many. Chance readers have told me of incidents in their lives which happened years before we met, and of which I knew nothing; but whose fading memories were agreeably revived by some of the verses here reprinted, when they met them in their flight through the newspapers as fugitive poetry.

This may serve for explanation and defence of the title I have chosen for this little rhythmic medley. To be sure, a keen-eyed inspector of specks may discover that, judging by my souvenirs of them, some things are memorized that are too trivial for commemoration even in this light way. But what is there in God's universe of atoms which is really trivial if we but give thought enough to find out what there is in and around it? And even with little thought a heart with a reasonable modicum of feeling may find something not to be lightly forgotten in that which an inspector of specks would pronounce trivial. Nevertheless I will confess that a few of these verses are of so trivial a nature that they would not have been given a place here except as memory-monitors. In that role now and then a reader may find for his own self as much in them as in poems of more pretense. At any rate there are so few of them that their introduction cannot give much offense.

Pittsfield, Mass., September, 1895.

SCATTER THE GERMS OF THE BEAUTIFUL.

Scatter diligently in susceptible minds
The germs of the good and the beautiful.
There trees will spring from them, to blossom
·And bear the golden fruit of Paradise.—*German Poem.*

Scatter the germs of the beautiful ;
  By the wayside let them fall,
That the rose may spring by the cottage side,
  And the vine on the garden wall.
Cover the rough and the rude of earth
  With a veil of leaves and flowers,
And strew with the opening bud and cup
  The path of the summer hours.

Scatter the germs of the beautiful
  In the holy shrine of home ;
Let the pure, the fair and the graceful there
  In their loveliest luster come ;
Leave not a trace of deformity
  In the temple of the heart,
But gather about its hearth the gems
  Of nature and of art.

Scatter the germs of the beautiful
  In the temples of our God ;
The God who starred the uplifted sky
  And flowered the trampled sod.

When he built a temple for himself
   And a home for his priestly race,
He reared each arch in symmetry
   And curved each line in grace.

Scatter the germs of the beautiful
   In the depths of the human soul ;
They shall blossom there and bear thee fruit
   While the endless ages roll.
Plant with the pure and beautiful
   This pathway to the tomb,
And the pure and fair about thy path
   In Paradise shall bloom.

THE STANDPOINT.

"Give me where to stand," was the ancient postulate "Find where to stand," says modern dissent. "STAND WHERE YOU ARE," said Goethe, "and move the world."—F. H. HEDGE.

From thy heart's still chambers gazing
  On the mad, vain world without,
Longing Heavenward to raise it,
  Art thou still perplexed with doubt?
Seekest thou a standing place
Whence to raise thy fallen race?

Stay thee, brother, seek no further;
  Stand and labor where thou art,
Know, there is no standpoint firmer
  Than a true man's steadfast heart;
Strengthened by all power above
Is thy spirit's human love!

Humble brother, cease repining
  That thou canst not banish wrong;
Up! it *is* in thee to crush it,
  Nought hath power to make thee strong
Like the hidden links that bind
  Thee to the lowest of thy kind!

Where the world's great heart is beating,
　　Wouldst thou wield a power divine?
Wouldst thou that its mighty throbbings
　　Beat in unison with thine?
Through the world's wide veins be poured,
The love within thy bossom stored!

Ask no might divine, supernal,
　　Strive as only mortal can,
Bethink thee Who from Heaven descended
　　To be one with mortal man:
So might the Monarch of the skies
Be touched with our infirmities.

Be thy zeal then meek, unscornful;
　　Stand not from thy kind apart;
Find the vantage ground thou seekest
　　In a pure and loving heart:
There, brave brother, do thy best,
With our Father leave the rest!

LIGHT UP.

[The banks and brokers of Wall street have found
that their safes and vaults are better protected by a
brilliant illumination of gas around them than by
massive window-shutters.—*New York paper.*]

Lo, the shadows of evening, murky and brown,
Creep up through the highways and lanes of the
    town ;
          Light up!

Pass the word through the marble arenas of pride,
Pass the word through the cellars where miseries
    hide ;
          Light up!

Deeds that are evil love the mantling of night,
Love the hiding of darkness—not the showing of
    light ;
          Light up!

Murder lurks low in the by-ways of earth,
And wicked things struggle to monstrous birth;
          Light up!

Let the radiance flash on the murderer's dirk,
It is dulled for the doing its terrible work ;
          Light up!

Let its crystal wall circle your coffers of gold,
They are safer than cased in stone triple-fold :
>> Light up !

And learn ye this lesson—and learn it aright :
In the soul, as the city, wrong fleeth the light :
>> Light up !

As the sinner shrinks back when the light shines
>> within,
From the light in the soul so shrinketh the sin ;
>> Light up !

School, pulpit and press—bold rostrum, true tongue,
Abroad let your radiant teachings be flung !
>> Light up !

And the evil that struggles to monstrous birth
Shall die in the soul ere it curses the earth :
>> Light up !

SUNNY VALE.—A STORY

One sunny summer afternoon,
Fairest in laughing, leafy June,
Happiest man beneath Heaven's dome
A farmer brought his young wife home;
And as they reached the mountain's brow
And saw his cottage smile below,
He bade his bonnie bride mark well
How gaily there the sunshine fell.

June came again.—A cradled child
Beneath the cottage roof-tree smiled:
So like the light from its blue eyes
To that which fell from June's blue skies,
Both seemed from the same Heaven to come
To mingle in the farmer's home.
Thus loved he to his wife to praise
The luster of those golden days.

June came again.—No child was there:
The cradle of its smiles was bare.
Yet, though the farmer's face was sad,
The grace of new-found peace it had.
He strove the mother's grief to calm,
And said the June days brought a balm;
For something more than sunbeams fell
From where their child had gone to dwell.

June came once more.—The farmer's wife
Was passing from this earthly life:
They laid her in our sunniest glade
Before its frailest flowers could fade.—
That year the farmer did not mark
If earth or sky were bright or dark:
Yet there the careless sunlight fell
Gaily as if all things were well.

June cometh now.   From scenes the dead
Had left too lorn, the farmer fled;
And strangers from his lonely hearth
Dispel the gloom with household mirth,
While not a tone in any voice
Says some have wept where they rejoice:
And still the blithesome sunshine falls
As gaily round those cottage walls.

IN GREYLOCK'S SHADOW.

Where the dale in Greylock's shadow lies,
  A myriad streamlets flow,
And, gliding on through grove and glade,
  In braided beauty glow.

How often on their emerald banks,
  At morn or sunset's hour,
We've gathered many a pleasant thought,
  And many a bue-eyed flower.

But, fading with the floweret's bloom,
  The pleasant thought is gone,
And we roam no more the streamlet side
  At sunset's hour or morn.

Yet the blushing wave as brightly now
  Reflects Aurora's rose ;
And, on the grassy banks, anew,
  As fair the violet grows.

There's many a laugh as glad as ours,
  And many a step as light,
And eyes as full of hope are turned
  On Greylock's mountain height.

But not to us comes back again,
  The hope that there was born,
And we roam no more the streamlet side
  At sunset hour or morn.

GREEN HILLS OF TAGHCONIC.

All sounds are hushed to silence
　　Save the insect's lulling drone,
And the murmur of the brooklet
　　O'er its bed of pebbled stone.
Far off the green hills of Taghconic
　　In the glow of the sunset lie,
Entwined with a chaplet of roses,
　　And clasped in the arms of the sky:
For round as the bosom of beauty
　　They swell from the vale in the west;
And catching the rose-hue of twilight,
　　Seem blushing to be caressed.

One cloudlet of silvery vapor,
　　That awhile on the hill-top hung,
Like a gossamer scarf by a maiden
　　O'er her fair young shoulders flung,
Is gone; for the sky, a right lover,
　　The beautiful wearer kissed,
And drew to himself for a token
　　The scarlet of silvery mist.
But, lo! for the token thus ravished,
　　Less fleeting is that he bestows;
For, see, on the brow of the mountain,
　　A star-gemmed diadem glows.

To-night, by earth and Heaven,
    Alike is love-lore taught,
And the air with the sweetest wisdom
    Of happiness is fraught.
Then come to our tryst in the gloaming,
    Our tryst by the whispering beech,
And we'll con the lessons duly
    That the sages of Nature teach,
While, near us, the clear Housatonic
    Meandering flows to the sea,
And sounds with the silence harmonic
    Are blended in melody.

ON ONOTA'S GRACEFUL SHORE.

A BALLAD OF THE TIMES THAT TRIED MEN'S SOULS.

On Onota's graceful shore
In heroic days of yore,
A noble dwelt, as brave and true
As ere chivalric ages knew.
Yet over no proud castle walls.
And in no proud baronial halls
Did any scutcheoned banner show
His lineage from the long ago.

This noble ruled a country store
On fair Onota's graceful shore.
His sires, true to man and God,
The Mayflower's hallowed deck had trod:
And looked he to stern Plymouth rock
As proudly for ancestral stock
As though heraldic lore could trace
To Runnymede his name and race.

On gilded helm or broidered breast,
No men at arms ere wore his crest;
But, ranged on fair Onota's shore,
A hundred freemen stoutly swore
To answer, be it day or night,
His trumpet call or beacon light,
And soldierly his word obey
On the impending battle-day.

On Onota's fruitful shore,
Broad lands he had; and more
In fertile regions, far and near.
To his heart they had been dear:
Forests for parks; fields for the plow;
Lawns where stately homes rise now.—
Had they been beyond the sea,
They had been a barony.

I doubt this noble ere had read,
Or by any chance heard said,
That English barons sold their lands
To furnish forth their arméd bands
To wrench from Moslem rule the sod
Where once the Savior's feet had trod;
Yet said he, like those knights of old,
"Take my lands and give me gold!"

"What are lands, but to the free?
This gold shall guard our liberty.
My gallant men shall fitly go
To meet the proud and scornful foe:
As fitly clad and armed as they,
On the swift-coming battle-day.—
No awkward squad that foe shall greet
But trained to give them welcome meet."

Thus armed and clad, they marched them down
To drive the foe from Boston town.
The patriot hosts there gathered fast;
But many a weary month was past

Ere Britain's frigates sailed away
From Boston's long beleaguered bay;
While soldiers' hunger grew more keen,
And the camp larder passing lean.

Up spake this noble leader then—
Great-hearted leader of brave men.—
"My men, so brave and true and good,
Shall lack no more for daily food,
While I have meat and grain in store
On fair Onota's fruitful shore.
Hither bring beeves and sheep, fruit and grain;
Nought from their needs will I retain."

Boston freed from tyrant sway,
In realms Canadian, far away
Onota's noble and his band
Fought to free that northern land:
Fought, and fought exceeding well,
Till great Montgomery bleeding fell.
Then came disaster and defeat;
Disgraceful failure and retreat.

But no dishonor stained the name
Or blurred Onota's noble's fame.
Under most ignoble chiefs,
Burdened by a patriot's griefs,
He died: not by a battling foeman's blow,
But by the soldier's deadlier foe—
The pestilence whose viewless sword
Buckler nor martial skill can ward.

LAKE ONOTA, GREYLOCK IN THE DISTANCE.

By Lake Champlain's historic wave
They made Onota's patriot's grave.—
Grand champion of freedom's cause,
His life given in his country's wars,
His wealth to help her sorest need,
What is this noble's grateful meed?
His memory on Onota's shore :
Only that and nothing more !

ONOTA AND ITS NOBLE.

I believe it is not now the custom to print side
by side with historical poems their counterparts or
originals in prose ; but Byron indulged freely in the
practice ; and it would seem that his example might
be followed by those whose verse stands even more
in need of such interpretation. And so I will avail
myself of the precedent so far as the ballad of
Onota's shore is concerned. The ballad and the
description of its scenery are true to the letter; as
I will endeavor to show in the plainest prose.

As to the scene of the story: When I first saw
Lake Onota, nearly fifty years ago, it at once struck
me as the most beautiful in America of which I had
any knowledge, either personally or by report. That
opinion I have ever since maintained with ever in-
creasing confidence. And, of the great number of
persons of taste, some of them of taste cultivated
by wide travel in picturesque regions—who have
viewed the lake and its associated landscapes with

me, not one has controverted that opinion; but all
have assented to it more or less demonstratively ac-
cording to their several temperaments: often with
rapturous expressions of delight.   At the time of my
first visit the lake was surrounded by woods and
farms, with a few plain farmhouses; and its outlines
were somewhat marred by rude or careless occupa-
tion.   Now these shores are chiefly the artistically
arranged and skillfully cared-for groves and ave-
nues, lawns and gardens attached to the country
residences of Henry C. Valentine and Wirt D.
Walker, who have omitted nothing that good taste
and liberal expenditure could effect to make them
beautiful.   Other handsome places adorn the borders of the lake; while much of the remainder is a
spacious public park belonging to the city of Pittsfield; for whose citizens and others it is an attractive popular resort, commanding exquisite views, and
every year itself becoming more charming.   Thus
all that marred the fair lake's shores has disap-
peared, or is rapidly disappearing, giving place to
such new charms as wealth and landscape art can
add to those conferred by nature.

The many views of the lake taken from various
standpoints by artists of distinction prove that my
estimate of it is fully shared by those most competent to judge.   One of these views, a favorite one,
looks northward to Greylock, while in the middle
ground in Lanesboro, five miles away, Constitution
Hill is seen, its crown shaven like a monk's.   Little

more than a mile to the west are some of the most
graceful dome-like summits of the Taconics,—a
mountain range nowhere excelled in grace.   In the
foreground rises a graceful knoll on which in the
French and Indian wars stood a fort of some im-
portance.   Beyond this a graceful promontory ex-
tends into the lake forming a conspicuous feature of
the graceful curves which on every side compel the
admiration of all beholders.   All is grace.   Graceful
is the one word which belongs to Lake Onota;
while the landscape in which it is set is not deficient
in grandeur.

The view here presented shows Apple-tree Point,
a locality further up the lake, full of old-time memories.   This view of the lake is much extolled of
late.

THE STORY OF THE BALLAD

Is as literally and minutely true as the grace at-
tributed to the lake shore is without exaggeration.
In all its essential points this was proved beyond
question before a committee of the National House
of Representatives by Senator Henry L. Dawes
when he was a member of that House.   I will recite
the facts as briefly and in as plain prose as I can.

Prior to the year 1775 the greater part of what
are now the grounds of Wirt D. Walker, was the
farm of David Noble,who had on its southern border,
facing West street, a dwelling, a country store and
some small manufactory.   In 1774 the Massachu-

setts Provincial Congress recommended the organ-
izing in the several towns of the Province of
companies of minute men; that is, men solemnly
pledged to respond without a single moment's delay
to any call to arms which might be rendered neces-
sary by an expected raid of the British troops in
Boston, like that which provoked the Battle of Lexington; or by any other movement which should
give the signal that the confidently anticipated conflict of arms between Great Britain and her American
colonies was commencing. One of the companies
formed in accordance with this recommendation of
the Congress was composed of the flower of the
youth of Pittsfield and Richmond; and David Noble
was chosen its captain. Twenty years before, he
had been a soldier in the French and Indian wars;
and in 1774 he was lieutenant of the ordinary
Pittsfield Militia Company then just reorganized in
anticipation of early active service. It was therefore
with competent skill as well as ardent zeal that he
thoroughly drilled his men.

On the first of September, 1774, a movement of
General Gage led to a false report that the British
troops in Boston were firing upon Charlestown, and
an alarm was sent throughout the Province. The
Revolutionary leaders probably availed themselves
of the exciting rumor to test the spirit of the people
and the reliability of the minute men. If so, the
result of their experiment must have given them confidence and courage; for it was said, although doubt-

less with some little exaggeration, that the next morning forty thousand armed men were on their way to defend or avenge their countrymen. In this affair the Pittsfield and Richmond company marched as far as Westfield before the call was countermanded. Captain Noble went on to the center of Revolutionary opinion and operations around Boston; that town being practically a British camp, or garrison. What he learned there of the close approach of the great conflict and the vastness of the issues involved in it inspired him with a generous patriotic enthusiasm and zeal that was manifested in a manner which I think is without a parallel in Revolutionary history.

Returning home, he sold two farms in Stephentown, N. Y., and one or two in Pittsfield, receiving pay for the former at least in gold. With the money obtained by this sacrifice of his property Captain Noble supplied his company with one hundred and thirty stand of arms and uniformed them in neat and substantial "regimentals;" their breeches being of buckskin and their coats " of blue turned up with white." To obtain the material for this, he went to Philadelphia, where he also hired a breeches-maker, who returned with him to Pittsfield, where the uniforms were made up, in his own house, during the winter.

The company thus generously equipped, drilled with corresponding zeal, and acquired an efficiency which it was soon called to exercise. The news of

the Battle of Lexington, or more probably the alarm
sent out by Paul Revere on the night preceding
what the Pittsfield records humorously call "the
excursion of the King's troops," reached Captain
Noble's company at noon on the twenty-first of April,
and at sunrise the next morning it had joined the
regiment of Colonel Patterson of Lenox, to which it
belonged, and was on its march to Cambridge. The
corps served well during the siege of Boston, and
on one occasion received the special commendation
and thanks of Washington in general orders. At
one time there was an almost famishing scarcity of
food in Captain Noble's camp, which he remedied
by sending orders to bring the large supply of pro-
visions in his store on the shore of Lake Onota, and
to have them hauled by his oxen which would
furnish beef, so that the necessities of his soldiers
were relieved, for a time at least.

The British garrison having evacuated Boston on
the seventeenth of March, Colonel Patterson's
regiment was sent, late in April, to re-enforce the
army then engaged in the second year of the attempt to conquer Canada; or, rather, to free it from
British rule. The project of this conquest was dear
to the hearts of the Pittsfield patriots, with whom it
originated; and a Berkshire Regiment had been
honorably prominent in the campaigning from the
first. All had gone well until the able and gallant
commander, General Montgomery, the idol of the
Berkshire soldiery, on the thirty-first of December,

1775, fell while leading an assault on Quebec. After that all was indecision and incompetence—with a possibility of treachery in one quarter: for Pittsfield's arch-enemy, the traitor Arnold, was one of the commanders. There was a little sharp fighting, in which they took part, after the arrival of Patterson's regiment; but early in May Burgoyne reached Quebec with a large force for its defence. The Americans were compelled to retire from before that city and soon to abandon Canada entirely. All that dash and enthusiasm, inspired by a reasonable hope of great results—in spite of imperfect discipline, meager numbers and the scantiest appointments—had enabled the army of 1775 to win, was lost in a few brief weeks of 1776.

The remnant of the retreating force reached Crown Point in June in a state of demoralization which is vividly depicted as follows in a letter of July 7, from John Adams, who then visited it:

"Our army at Crown Point is an object of wretchedness enough to fill a humane mind with horror; disgraced, defeated, discontented, dispirited, diseased, naked, undisciplined, eaten up with vermin; no clothes, beds or blankets: no medicine; no victuals but salt pork and flour. I hope that measures will be taken to cleanse our army at Crown Point of smallpox."

Captain Noble had, on the first of July written thus: "Our army is very much distressed by reason of the smallpox. We have had four thousand sick

at one time. The distress of our sick is such that
I cannot paint it out by pen and ink. * * * All
my companions have had it."

He had himself had the smallpox, and supposed
that he had recovered; but he died from the second-
ary effects of the dread disease shortly after his
letter was written; and he was buried on the shore
of Lake Champlain.

Such is the plain unvarnished tale of the generous,
truehearted and gallant noble of Lake Onota's
graceful shore. Is it not a memory worthy a
souvenir?

OUR FATHERS' CHURCH.

Our fathers' church—this gray old church
  That stands on the oak-crowned hill;
What visioned things this twilight brings
  Its ruined porch to fill;
How forms will throng from slumbers long
  In memory's chambers dim ;
How music flows whose sweet death-close
  Passed into Heaven's hymn.
Oh tender memories that dwell
  Around these time-stained walls,
The rapt heart, answering to your spell,
  All vanished things recalls.

'Mid this oak wood, that gray church stood
  In Sabbath hours of old ;
Its spire arose through winter snows,
  And summer clouds of gold.
No silver chime tolled holy time ;
  No rolling organ pealed;
No sun's rich beams, in mellowed gleams,
  Fell round us as we kneeled ;
But down those aisles, with quiet smiles,
  Our white-haired fathers came,
And, as we knelt, our hearts we felt
  Fired by their spirit's flame.

That dear old shrine! not all divine
   The early joys it knew,—
For oft we made its ample shade
   Our summer rendezvous;
And oft the flood of youth's hot blood,
   Matched with the wintry blast;
What starry nights, in slippery flights,
   We down yon hill sped fast.—
There still, in June's sweet afternoons,
   We lie in mood serene,
And half of shade our reveries braid,
   And half of fairest sheen.

That green-sloped lawn! at flush of dawn,
   Or gentler fall of even,
With faltering word—more guessed than heard,
   Fond vows have there been given.
The light is gone from eyes that shone;
   The fire from hearts aflame :—
Nay! hide it now, if perjured vow
   Hath helped their glow to tame;
Young hearts meet yet, where lovers met
   At twilight years ago,
And deem it well, old joys to tell,
   And not the olden woe.

Yon gray old church, that stands apart,
   Deserted—half o'erthrown—
It hath all power, in this still hour,
   To summon what hath flown.

A costlier fane—God's fitter shrine,
　　They say our feet have found;
And where our sires lit altar fires,
　　No more is holy ground.
But pride ne'er bows, nor passion stills,
　　As when we wander there;
For holiest consecration fills
　　Our Fathers' house of prayer!

OUR ANCIENT VILLAGE BURIAL GROUND.

Amid our new and bustling town,
　　The ancient village graveyard lies,
Its paths with broken marbles strewn,
　　O'er-wept by no fond mourner's eyes;
　　Its olden limits half o'ergrown
By grim brick walls that, blank and bare,
Out on the trampled hillocks glare.

The schoolboy here with noisy zest
　　Pursues his sport; nor checks his mirth
To fancy that the shadows rest
　　More darkly than on other earth;
　　Yet slow, sad feet each turf have prest,
And—water blessed of sorrow's God—
Love's tears have hallowed every clod.

Here now funereal tears ne'er flow;
 The weepers weep not where they wept.
The swelling tide of human woe
 Beyond the olden grief hath swept.
 Of those who died so long ago,
The sculptured marble o'er their graves
Only a strange, vague memory saves.

Yet sometimes off a crumbling stone
 The garrulous graybeard scans a name,
And tells the listener it was one
 That had its little hour of fame :
 That, for some public service done
Was by the country folk revered ;
Or for some austere power was feared.

The rose is gone whose gentle bloom
 Showed dust somewhat more dear to love,
Than that whose proud and stately tomb,
 The colder marble gleamed above :
 And men may muse if ghastlier doom
The broken tomb of greatness shows,
Or beauty's with its uptorn rose.

Awhile yon little copse yet stands :
 'Twas planted, one long-vanished year,
By those who, seeking far-off lands,
 Buried their richest treasures here.—
 They deemed, like harps in spirit hands,
These wind-swept trees would long complain ;
But not how lorn would be their strain.

And thus our ancient burial place
  Within its shrinking borders holds
But here and there a fading trace
  Of those whose dust its dust enfolds.
  The ranks of life advance apace :
The majesty of Death in vain
Keeps ward with all his spectral train.

Within this ancient burial ground,
  The fathers rest in slumbers deep,
As heedless of the turmoil round
  As the mad crowd of their sweet sleep
  Yet hath the reverent muser found,
The grave of Eld hath even here,
Grand voices for the willing ear.

AFTER THE KNELL.

Hic quiescit qui nunquam quievit.

Here then where willows sigh around,
   Worn one, thou sleepest well:
Thy heart of fire at length hath found
   Its only soothing spell.
Thou'lt rest; best lullaby yon bell's slow chime
   That pealed for thee the evening song of time.

Each clarion hope that roused thy youth
   Hath ceased its trumpet clang.
Love's lyre is stilled; and stilled—sad sooth—
   Love's voice that sweeter sang;
Thou'lt rest; thine ear's quick sense so cold and dull
   Though Myra sang, she could nor fire nor lull.

Each phantom gleam thy feet pursued
   In calmest night expires;
No more for thee shall be renewed
   Their soul-deceiving fires:
Blest lullaby yon bell's slow chime
   That sang for thee the evening hymn of time.

VOICES FROM OCEAN.

Comes there no voice upon the landward breeze—
No blessed tidings in the sound of seas?
Far rolls our lay—echo its call prolongs;
Comes there to shore no answer to our songs?
List, list again! oh, listen with your heart!
Fancy may yet some joyous thrill impart!

Look o'er yon wave; along its whitening crest.
What gleams afar in light and beauty drest?
Doth our lost bark again come wandering home?
Vainly we dream,—'tis but the flashing foam.
Yet gaze again; shine, star of Hope, once more
Compel the waste our loved ones to restore!

Thus we look out across the wildering waves,
And claim our dear ones from their far-off graves;
Thus wildly chide the ocean's rocky bed
That coldly clasps our bosom-cherished dead.
In vain! yet who the impassioned dream would
    break,
And unto long, dull, hopeless agony awake?

Thus we look out across Life's wildering sea,
And pray for that we know may never be;
Thus do we sit and list at even fall,
Waiting for tones we know are silent all;
Yet coldest Reason, spare our dreams thy chill
Till thou their place with better radiance fill!

GIVE FANCY PLAY.

"Halloo! my Fancy, whither wilt thou stray?"—*Old Poem.*

Down the long path thro' the Future that lies,
        Let Fancy stray!
Fair hills, o'er fair valleys, in fair vistas rise,
        Joy-lighted to-day;
'Tis beyond them life's night-dews in teardrops shall
    fall,
When the gloaming of age casts its shade over all.
Will the dis-gilded landscape your bosom enthrall
        When the twilight grows gray?

Whence shall the darkness enshadow your brow?
        Let Fancy say!
Which of your treasures are marked, even now,
        With the sign of decay?
Sunflashing your tresses now float on the air;
What are the sorrows shall silver that hair?—
Shall fierce joy, oh rare blusher, pang'd pain, or dull
    care
        Pale your rose-tint away?

Sunny or dark be the wing that she plume,
        Give Fancy play!
What are the flowers whose summerly bloom
        Shall be sweet round your way!

Where on your pathway shall memory fling
Light round the spots where your heart's love shall
    cling?
Where are the founts whence your tear-drops shall
    spring?

      Would Fancy but say!

LAY OF THE PAPER-RAG CUTTER.

Souvenirs of many a life,
Shreds with many a mystery rife,
Odds and ends from many lands
To the rag girl's busy hands,
Torn and soiled, are hither brought.
Waking many a curious thought,
As, with wondering guess and dream,
She rends the web and rips the seam.

This—the embroidered emblems show—
Wrapped, as in folds of heaven's own snow,
A child as pure, when Luxury's heir
Was vowed to Heaven with rite and prayer.
Grew he as pure as robe and vow?
Or world-stained as these shreds are now?
Nay; whatsoe'er we know or dream,
We rend the web and rip the seam.

This :   Beneath its virgin white,
On some far-off wedding night,
A bride's heart beat as pure and glad
As the bright vesture that her clad.—
Dwells that heart still secure in bliss?
Or trampled, torn and stained, like this?
Ah, whatsoe'er we know or dream,
We rend the web and rip the seam.

This :   By stranger's fingers bound
To the soldier's gaping wound,
It drank the life-blood of the brave,
Destined to an unknown grave.—
His name : is it saved in the saved land,
Or cast away, like this stained band?
Nay, whatsoe'er we know or dream,
We rend the web and rip the seam.

This :   Age on age hath passed away,
With conqueror after conqueror's sway
Since first it swathed a mummied thing
That once perchance had been a king.—
The thing itself hath food supplied
For Arab fires or Savan's pride ;
And whatsoe'er we know or dream,
We rend the web and rip the seam.

But what boots it to surmise
Tales that with each fragment rise?
Beggar's tatters, robes of state,
Fashion's fripperies out of date.

Widow's garments, worn and thin,
Tawdry gauds, the garb of sin ;
All are hither mingled brought
With a thousand fancies fraught ;
And whatsoe'er we know or dream,
We rend the web and rip the seam.

All heedless of their first estate,
Commingled in one common fate,
In shapeless piles —the robes of pride,
Rags, scant gaunt squalor's form to hide,
Priestly vestments, gauds of sin,
(Their conflict o'er men's souls to win)
The garbs of joy, the garbs of woe,
Hence to the vat of cleansing go—
Earth-befouled, their old life spent ;
Into countless shreddings rent.
Thence they shall come forth again
Without tinge of blot or stain,
Purged by cunning alchemy
Into spotless purity.
Crushed and pressed with iron strength,
Yea, they shall come forth at length,
Fit in their new estate to bear
Truth's purest thought, Love's purest prayer.
Then, whatsoe'er we know or dream,
O rend the web and rip the seam.

Pure once as hues that them bedight
In token of fair souls as white,

Perchance, ere life's dread march was o'er,
Some soiling came to those who wore
(Such things are told in many a tale)
The christening robe, the bridal veil,
The soldier's plume, the Egyptian crown.
Perchance they to the grave went down,
Sin-soiled in soul, with crushed, rent hearts,
Pierced through with guilt's envenomed darts.
What then?   Is there no alchemy divine,
In Heaven no cleansing power benign,
That the sin-soiled again may be
Restored to pristine purity?
Fails then God's all-embracing might
In power to wash all stained souls white,
And from His vat of cleansing raise
Pure hearts whereon to write His praise?
As thus we muse and thus we dream,
We rend the web and rip the seam.

OUR CHARITY.

"Judge not thy brother," saith the Christ,
"Lest thine the doom thou givest;
If God were swift in wrath thou diest,
He pities and thou livest.
For thine own guilt let grief begin,
Another's fault deferring;
Let him among you free from sin,
The first condemn the erring."

The Christ hath said, and we reply—
"See, Lord, our guilty brother!
The sin that crieth to the sky
Belongeth to another."
Forgetful that for us the sword
By grace alone delayeth,
We murmur that the righteous Lord
So long his vengeance stayeth.

We try the reins, we search the heart,
We doom the high and lowly;
Our sin-blind eyes assume the part
Of Judgment, as the Holy.
We see our neighbor's close intent,
We grasp his inmost feeling—
Scant cloak of charity is lent
His guiltiness concealing!

The poor man of the rich man's pride,
　　And miser greed, complaineth,
And crieth, " Thou for all who died,
　　This man thy child disdaineth."
The rich man, in life's Sabbath pause,
　　For pauper error prayeth,
And, most of all God's holy laws,
" Thou shalt not steal," he sayeth.

The iron saint, of visage stern,
　　Frowns on all joyous laughter,
And prays that pleasure's toils may earn
　　An endless woe hereafter.
The galliard, gay and debonair,
　　All saintly words deriding,
Counts them but Pharisaic prayer,
　　And Puritanic chiding.

The foe beholds from wisdom's way,
　　His foeman's footsteps vary,
And marks each devious step astray,
　　As hunter marks his quarry,
But while, with gloating gaze intent :
　　He follows all unheeding,
He deemeth not his feet are bent
　　Upon the same misleading.

And friend marks friend with jealous eye,
　　Some curious plan devising,
Each fault and foible to espy,
　　The better by surprising.

The tortured bosom feels the gaze
　Of friendship on it burning,—
Perchance the seeker goes his ways,
　No happier for his learning.

And each frail judge, presumption strong
　Of frail material weaving,
Is sure to do his neighbor wrong;
　Mayhap past all retrieving.
Some prayer-told plea, unheard by man,
　Some saving thought unheeded,
Our human weakness fails to scan,
　For Godlike judgment needed.

Oh Thou, whose eye alone can reach
　The bosom's inmost feeling,
To us our secret errors teach;
　Self to itself revealing.
Thy word is just, Thy judgment sure,
　Thy glance all-comprehending;
Search Thou our hearts, and make them pure,
　Thy grace upon us sending.

Oh, Thou who givest every grace,
　Give us that grace abiding,
That love may all our hate efface,
　Our neighbor's weakness hiding.
Plant the sweet flower, Charity,
　Deep in the hearts within us,
And let its precious perfume be
　A charm for Heaven to win us!

SHE HATH BEEN FAIR.

Haggard, withered and gaunt, she sat crooning by
the churchyard path; her thin white hair ruffled
by the evening breeze; her long, almost fleshless
fingers clutching convulsively the coarse grass that
grew rank above a sunken grave—the grave of a
child: but they said "she had been fair."

Mid sunken graves she sits, alone;
A wan and worn and haggard crone,
With strange-set eyes whose cavernous glare
      All joy hath flown:
And yet, they say " she hath been fair."

At rarest feasts her praises rung,
While raptured men around her clung:
For love himself had made his lair.
      Young poets sung—
Amid the mazes of her hair.

If that the fond, enamored youth
Have limned in song no more than truth—
Man's frailest songs maid's frailer charms outwear—
      I think in sooth
That she was something more than fair.

Love's tremulous arms, close-clasped and warm,
Thrilled with their thrill that withered form;
On those thin lips his kisses rained
     In passion's storm,
While there he deemed his heaven was gained.

Nay, more: upon that shriveled breast,
Lulled by her songs to balmiest rest,
Once laughed in sleep love's fairest child,
     While she, half blest,
By fitful changes, wept and smiled.

And now she walks the world, alone,
A mateless, childless, wildered crone;
Dear God, should memory ere recall
     What she hath known,
How must the ghost her soul appall!

That ghost must rise.   Youth falsely deems
The heart forgets its early dreams—
The loves, the prides with which our May
     So thickly teems—
Because the glossy hair grows gray.

No, no! even now, from rill or bird,
Yon wrinkled creature's fancy heard
The words that, in her young ear poured,
     Sweet rapture stirred,
When flattery long ago adored.

Ah, little know ye of the thought
From which the dream of age is wrought,
The pangs with which the glance it throws
      O'er life, is fraught,
Though calm as sunsets seem its close.

June's suns upon December's snow
The blighting of their splendor throw.
Out of the joyous glittering past,
      A sudden glow,
Charged with some strange weird spell, is cast.

But she, with scared back-glancing eyes,
Naught but a storm-wrecked past descries :
Tempestuous joy, stormy delight :
      Then wild-wailed sighs,
Tempestuous gloom and rayless night.

Till now—as from all loathsome harms—
Maids who outstretch their round, white arms,
In charity, shrink from her grasp,
      Whose fairer charms
Love held in maddest passion-clasp.

"The poor old thing is crazed," they say :
"When our night revelry is gay,
She haunts, anear, the cold street stones ;
      Mumbling, all day
Above a shrunken grave she crones."

" She crones o'er graves :" why should she shrink
From the Death-chasm's crumbling brink ?
Less dread the gleams from graves that rise,
  In graves to sink,
Than loveless light from sunniest eyes.

Shield Thou the stricken of Thy rod,
Shield from scorn's idle pity, God,
And in Thy one sure refuge hide,
  Beneath the sod,
Distorted beauty ; broken pride.

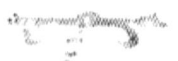

MEMORIES OF THE YEAR.

"And this our life, exempt from public haunt,
Finds tongues in trees."—*As You Like It.*

Dost remember the array
  Of the laughing forest trees ;
In the merry month of May
  How they quivered in the breeze ?
Quivered as a happy boy
Trembles with some new-found joy.
How elastic where we trod
Sprang the mossy, flowered sod !
More elastic sprang our hearts
From the footprints time imparts.

Then a myriad snow-white blossoms
Decked the cherry, as a maid
For her bridals is arrayed.
Even the patriarchal pine
Wore a grandeur more benign,
Smiling to the Spring's caress
As a grandsire is beguiled
Into laughter by a child.

    Dost remember
          How the splendors
Of the spring began to fade
  When the cherry's bridal blossoms
Stained and scattered strewed the glade ?

How in Summer's sultry solstice
All the freshness left the leaf,
  As the fresh fair cheek is withered
By life's sultrier joy or grief?

O'er the gaudier flowers of summer,
  Still they clung upon the bough,
While Spring's fair and fragile daughters
  Slept in early graves below.—
So we human mourners linger
O'er the tombs of those we mourn;
With a smile of mocking likeness—
Likeness in a strange unlikeness—
To the smiles our young lips wore
Answering lips that smile no more.

  Dost remember
            In the sober
Autumn splendor of October,
  How the tempest-maddened gale,
Rent the many-colored garments
  From the hilltop and the vale?
Then the gorgeous flowers of summer,
Like the gentle flowers of spring,
Perished and in thousands fell,
In the garden and the dell.

  Dost remember
In this dark and drear December?

Lo, the crisp leaves, scant and sear,
  Shiver in the tempest's rage,
As old men whose end is near
  Tremble with the woes of age.

Still the grandly changeless pines
  In the solemn loneness rise,
Over Nature's ruined shrines
  Pointing spire-like to the skies.
Waiting in calm faith they stand
  Till the Builder shall repair
Every temple of His hand :
  All the broken arches there.

Like the fragile flowers of spring
  Youthful pleasure fades and dies.
Time and change their blighting bring
  To ambition's gaudier prize.

Mid a lifetime's scattered ruins,
  Virtue standeth like the pine.
In a patient faith abiding :
  Waiting with a hope divine ;
Knowing that the Perfect Giver,
  For each lost imperfect joy,
Will restore a purer pleasure,
  Heavenly and without alloy ;
For each glory that ambition
  In his proudest hour has known.
He a loftier aspiration
  With a nobler wreath shall crown.

NAY, NEVER LIGHTLY TELL THE TALE.

Nay, never lightly tell the tale
   When crime his doom shall bear,
For hearts that spurned the guilty joy,
   The agony must share.
There's not a pang which justice
   On sin most rightly deals,
But all its poisoned keenness,
   Some guileless bosom feels.

And scorn not thou the new-born tear
   From sin-dried fount that flows ;
A dream of fond hearts wronged and crushed
   May well that fount unclose ;
For men who brave undaunted,
   The sword that justice wears,
Shall faint and shrink and tremble
   For fates enlinked with theirs.

So thick the twined affections
   Around all bosoms cling,
The blow one chord that striketh,
   A thousand hearts may wring.
Then think when paths invite thee,
   With guilty gladness strown,
The end is dark with sorrow,
   Thou shalt not meet alone.

NOW CROWN THE CONQUEROR TIME !

A NEW YEAR'S LYRIC.

Now crown the Monarch Time !
Who cometh from the myriad fields of fame,
    In conquering might sublime :
All fadeless glories clustering round his name ;
The spoils from Earth's historic empires torn,
Before his iron car, triumphal trophies, borne !

    Hero and statesman built
Empurpled annals up to glory's height ;
    Theirs still the blood and guilt ;
All else adorns the triumph of his might,
Who comes from havoc wider than they made,
A conqueror in their spoiled royalties arrayed.

    He wears the Cæsar's wreath
—Though scant to veil the breadth of his bald
    brow—
    And, not to thoughts that breathe,
But to his hollow tones Rome's forum echoes now,
Yea, templed Greece,—once egotist divine—
No other wreath than his hangs on each ruined
    shrine !

Nor did the Pharaoh raise
Pyramidal or mystic sculptured mass
　　To his own paltry praise :
But all to him whose sceptre was the hour glass ;
Who kept even then his royal state alone
In chambers where the Assyrian built his throne.

　　Time reigneth well o'er all !
Go read his annals on each crumbling tower
　　That tells a tyrant's fall ;
Nor less in ancient Albion's storied power,
And young Columbia's blazonry of strength.
Time bids the good prevail, and brings the best at
　　length.

　　He reigneth well o'er Earth,
And lightens in her fields the peasant's toil.
　　Her rocks of sterile dearth
He mellows to the soft and grateful soil.
Yes, Earth is greener for his genial reign,—
More luscious her pulped fruits ; more golden her
　　ripe grain !

　　Then crown the Monarch Time,
Whose reign is over fields and towers and thrones,
　　From Earth's star-welcomed prime !
Ye towns unwalled with Time-defying stones,
Ye empires strong, while loyal to your king,
Your homage and your shouts to his new crowning
　　bring !

And come ye serried hills.
That yearly lay your leafy tiaras down,
        And not until he wills,
Assume again the tributary crown !
And you, ye mountains, come, or helmed with
        snows,
Or nodding your plumed fires above your wrinkled
        brows !

Thou, Ocean, homage pay !
Time's coral isles invade thine ancient realm :
        He claimeth from thy prey
A tithe of all which thou dost overwhelm ;
Thy kingdom ends when he shall be no more ;
God's angel plants his foot on thee, as on the shore !

        Ye radiant hosts of night,
Sing—as ye sang to hail his mighty birth—
        His arm's victorious might,
His power imperial, and his royal worth !
Join our bright pageant with your gorgeous train,
And swell our anthem peal with your exultant
        strain !

        And thou, oh Monarch Sun,
Who metest out our monarch's circling days
        Smile thou on what is done !
Pour, over all, thy bright and genial rays,
As many an hour thou dost, till mortals deem
Heaven's blessing falls in every golden beam.

We crown the Monarch Time !
Peal festal chimes from old cathedral towers,
    And spires he makes sublime
With mosses gray—his heralds of the hours ;
But gladder changes ring on village bells,
That wake the new-born echoes of our forest dells !

    To deck our peerless king,
No outworn diadem of Tyranny,
    No triple tiara bring !
Nor iron crown revered, of Lombardy :
No purples moldy with the world's old dew,
For him whose conquest is the past, whose realm the
    new.

    But thou, my country, bind
The clustering stars of thy fresh springing states,
    In one fair circlet twined,
Around his brow who thy new crowning waits ;
And pray that, in that band of living light,
The glow grow ever purer and the gleam more
    bright.

    Aye, bring, for royal robe,
Nought but our flag's celestial panoply,—
    For all sceptred globe
Our Eagle ! Lo, uplifted to the sky,
Our free old mountains wait him for sole throne,
That never king before hath ruled or sat upon !

We crown thee, royal Time !
Oh, reign not as the conqueror reigns,
    Smile on thy willing clime ;
Change thou the wrong which from of old remains ;
Not as the rifted rock to thy strong earthquake
    yields,
But as thy genial springs make smooth the rude
    new fields !
    January 1, 1857.

DEDICATORY PROLOGUE.

PITTSFIELD ACADEMY OF MUSIC, DECEMBER 16, 1872.

Recited by the Leading Actress.

The spell is cast.   Behind its painted wall
The magic pageant waits the master's call !
Yet for a while, in his impatient hand,
Unlifted rests the wizard's potent wand.
Something he lacks.   His sorcery's charms at fault,
All incomplete his incantations halt.
We need invoke in the old rhythmic way
To this fair realm that craves their genial sway,
The mighty muses that in every age
Have shed their influence on the mimic stage.

Thou proud, dark mistress of the tragic art,
At whose strong bidding all our tears upstart :
In whose stern scenes, from others' woes we win
The knowledge that by suffering entereth in ;
In thy grand crowning, sorrow, throned sublime,
Rebukes more royally even royal crime.
Thine are the pangs which godlike natures know—
Triumphant agony ; the majesty of woe ;
Thine the fierce furies whose relentless feet
Pursue the murderer's step with vengeance meet.
Queen of Life's loftiest thought, Death's tenderest
　　ruth,
Thou dark veiled teacher of ennobling truth,
Come from the boards where thou each changing
　　scene
Wast wont to tread with Garrick. Kemble, Kean ;
Where grew the fame our fresh-mourned Forrest
　　gained,
Where Linley charmed, and royal Siddons reigned ;
Where she, the Kemble of our Berkshire Hills,
Almost even now, enchants, and awes, and thrills.
From each old memory-haunted green-room bring
　　with thee
For us, a dream of memories yet to be !

Thou too, quaint wearer of the comic mask,
Whose " fierce endeavor " and appointed task,
It is, to exorcise our follies with a laugh.
No bitter draught thou bidst thy patients quaff,
But curest all our humors, half our ills,
With Dr. Momus' sugar-coated pills.

'Gainst vice and folly, wit's a sovereign balm,
That works, to quote friend Renne, "like a charm."
Royal physician, conqueror of all pain,
Oh, " Stoop to conquer," in this new domain.

And thou, bright ruler of the choral dance,
Whose waving arms and flashed imperial glance
The soft-eyed houris of the fair ballet
In twining wreaths and circling grace obey,
Muse of the mazy step and dazzling zone,
Each bosom yields to thee a willing throne ;
Foes thou may'st have in temples more austere,
But surely none but loyal lovers here.

Muse of the quivering lyre and minstrel's song,
Slaves to whose power the captive passions throng,
Oh, show us here the drama's rapturous rage,
The gorgeous glories of the lyric stage !
With Handel bid us grandly to adore,
With Nillson thrill, with glorious Lucca soar !
Nor be forgot the mirthful sons of glee,
But let us laugh with laughing Barnabee !

Our charm is said, our invocation made !
Shall we receive, my friends, your voice's aid ?
Perhaps you think these mystic rites a "hum."
    Well :
On that point, then, I've something more to tell :
Our modern sages—very wise are they,
In the new wisdom of this latter day—

Deem that in every dead and dry old myth
There is a very juicy, living pith ;
That every hollow heathen god is packed
With a most solid mass of Christian fact ;
In short, that what the silly herd call silly lies,
Are great symbolic truths in Wisdom's eyes.

Now, if this learned philosophy be true,
We'll find our muses, smiling friends, in you :
And, as you bid us paint the tragic tale,
Or, with Wit's arrows, Folly's brood impale,
Or tread in Fairy dance the chalk-marked floor,
In you by turns each mythic patron we adore.
Yet, mythic or human, with no flatterer's guile
Can the stage court its patrons' favoring smile ;
Our task, to hold—I think the phrase is new—
The mirror up to nature, and to you :
And, well I ween, not every feature there
Is pictured grandly good, or purely fair.
No dame—nor e'en the sweetest, winsome lass
Can " handsome " always in her looking glass.

The self-same passions, virtues, vices, lurk
In Christian, Pagan, Jew and turbaned Turk.
The foreign garb is but polite disguise,
And won't deceive your penetrating eyes.
In heroes, lovers, even in fays and elves,
We paint, in very truth, your very selves.
Each week your Schools for Scandal duly meet,
Where tongues and needles in their speed compete.

Nay, smile not brothers : how about your club ?
Do reputations there ne'er get a rub ?
Ah, gentle brothers, very much I fear
That woman's foibles oft wear manly gear !

Enough ! to you who love the genial art.
That here uplifts the soul and melts the heart,
That scathes our follies and rebukes our faults,
Teaches, refines, ennobles and exalts ;
To you we dedicate, whate'er the rites,
This fairest temple of all fair delights.
In long procession, 'neath its gilded dome.
Through the bright portals of its stage, shall come
To you, the changeful drama's glittering train,
The Houris' dance, the Songstress' thrilling strain.
Yours are its splendors, yours its joys shall be :
Yours, too, to make, or mar, its destiny !

THE DESERTED BALL ROOM.

How hollow through the silence
　　Of this vacant festal hall,
Ring the echoes, oft-repeated,
　　Of our footsteps' lightest fall !
Hollow, lone, sad, repeated,
　　Sound they on this dance-worn floor ;
Like the memories of that night, love,
　　When we met here before.

Flashed joyous, in the flashing
　　Of a hundred tapers' blaze,
Glad eyes, ah, well remembered !
　　That have paled their joy-lit rays ;
And thrilling strains re-echoed—
　　Memory-echoed evermore—
Through this rose-wreathed hall, love,
　　When we met here before.

Stilled, like ceased music, the glad voices,
　　In life's stifling or the tomb ;
And ghostly echoes, only,
　　Haunt this empty festal room.
Hollow, thus, lone, sad, repeated,
　　Sound our footsteps on this floor ;
Bringing memories of that night, love,
　　When we met here before !

LIFE'S MORNING STARS.

We mourn the eyes that answered ours
   In pleasant days long gone:
Mild orbs that shone Life's morning stars,
   And faded with its dawn.
From other eyes, joy, genius, wit
   May flash their kindling powers;
But still we yearn for those which fell
   More lovingly on ours!

And still in dreams we meet their gaze
   When gloom the soul enshrouds;
The radiant stars of hope that break
   Through sorrow's rifted clouds.
Whoe'er may frown whose smiles should cheer
   When angry fortune glowers,
We know what pitying eyes would fall
   More lovingly on ours.

When light from all Life's broad serene,
   To us and ours is given,
When Earth and Earth-born things reflect
   The golden smile of Heaven;
From light that blackens into gloom
   Let but a cloudlet lower.
We turn to that whose brightest rays
   Illumed our darkest hour.

In Fancy's ken, still, still. those eyes
    Our cynosure shall gleam ;
Dear orbs that shone Life's morning stars
    Its stars of eve shall beam. —
And, aye, if Heaven at length we reach,
    Even in Heaven's love-blest bowers,
We know what waiting eyes will fall
    Most lovingly on ours.

MUSIC AT THE TWILIGHT HOUR.

Take the harp thine art devotes
     To soothing strains as night descends,
And, while zephyr round us floats,
     O sing the vesper song that blends
So sweetly with its notes,
     Till our bosoms own the power
     Of music at the twilight hour.

Take thy harp, fair queen of song,
     And let thy soul-sped fingers sweep
Its tremulous chords along,
     'Twill bid faint hearts with hope to leap,
Again with faith grow strong,
     While with tears they bless the power
     Music wields at twilight's hour.

Take thy harp while daylight dies,
     And sing the song whose magic strain
Bids all fond memories rise,
     And to our hearts bring back again
Dear tones from Paradise.
     Wield, oh wield the hallowed power
     Of music at the twilight hour.

THE VERMEIL LIP IS VICTRESS STILL.

Ho ! preachers of a dullard's cant,
   You press your prosy creed in vain ;
The plainly good doth not prevail,
   And Beauty's empire doth not wane :
Of homely graces prate who will,
The vermeil lip is victress still !

We chant our song to woman's power
   Still in the old poetic phrase—
The azure eye, the golden tress
   Are strong as in the ancient days ;
Not one of all the hues grows faint
That classic genius glowed to paint.

With Milton's gorgeous iris tints
   You deck your own young bosom queen,
And Shakespeare drew the counterpart
   Of her you lingered by yestreen ;
You deem, in fair Miranda's shrine
The indwelling soul *must* be divine.

Still Beauty triumphs in the thronged
   And fierce encounters of the dance ;
And still the heedless straggler falls
   Before some ambushed wayside glance :
Victress, where'er she flash her darts,
Still Beauty's Queen is Queen of Hearts !

OUR HUNTING MORN—AT EVE.

Up! our hunting morn is peeping
   As the evening twilight dies;
Let the dews suffice for weeping
   And the night wind for all sighs!

Hark! the hunt is onward flying,
   And the game is Love and Joy;
With Time, the hoary hunter, vieing
   Let us join the chase, my boy!

Coyest Love may be abiding—
   Where to say we hardly dare—
But we'll trace him to his hiding,
   Even in his snowiest lair!

Oh! be sure, if there we've found him,
   Though our trembling prize be coy,
If we've caught young Love, and bound him,
   Then we can't be far from Joy!

THE BREAKING OF LOVE'S DREAM.

A VERY MOURNFUL BALLAD.

The night was glorious—such an one
  As, clothed in virgin white,
When the long prosy day is done,
  Sets all the loves aflight.

The moon in Heaven's sapphire hung
  Amid her bright-eyed daughters,
And low her trembling image flung
  Upon the rippling waters.

And—*apropos*—for one so chaste—
  The very queen of prudes—
Diana has a queerish taste
  For kissing waves and woods.

Well, well! I hear a man is seen
  Quite often in her car;
Venus and she were quite too thick
  When V. was evening star.

And then she sheds such trait'rous light
  To cheat one's prudent fear;
While all around seems dazzling bright,
  Such shadows overnear!

'Twas so that night—that glorious one,
    The very cream of June,
When lovers thought their walk was done
    At least an hour too soon.

Paul stood within a shadow dim
    Before a mansion gate,
With one whose love was more to him
    Than all her Pa's estate.

He said so—while, with passion fraught,
    Love fired his trembling tongue,
And she Love's inspiration caught
    And on his accents hung.

But suddenly a voice rose there—
    A voice of woman old,
Loud shrieking on the startled air,
    " *Darter! come in this minnit, child—you'll
ketch your death a-cold!*"

A VALENTINE.

FROM TWO COLLIERS OF NEW ASHFORD TO TWO DAMSELS OF LANESBORO'.

Two brother collier chaps be we,
   Eke of New Ashford town,
Who oft two lovely damsels see,
   When we with coal come down.

And like our coal pits are our hearts,
   With love for you on fire,
When, sitting on our long black carts,
   Your beauty we admire.

And if our soot your taste don't suit,
   And you our suit despise,
Then like dead coals shall be our souls,
   As like live coals your eyes.

About our hue you needn't raise
   A mighty hue and cry;
It—like the hues some lovers praise,—
   Not quite skin deep doth lie.

And, ere we'll die for that dark dye,
   And perish of your scorn,
Soaked in weak lye a week we'll lie,
   Till white as we were born.

Nay,—though our skins were really black,—
  We never did get blue,
As ah! alas! and ah, good lack!
  Too many people do.

And thus, in this most tender lay,
  We lay our bosoms bare,
All in a way we hope will weigh,
  Against the hues we wear.

Oh! if you take the tender hearts,
  That we now tender you,
Away shall fly our heavy smarts,
  As smoke flies up the flue.

Gladly for you we'd change our hue,
  But if you say us nay,
We can but do, as doth the dew,
  And weep ourselves away.

Then, though for you in vain we've sued,
  Still o'er our graves a weeping yew
Shall say that us, though never slewed,
  Two cruel maidens slew.

WINTER ELFINRY.

THE MARVELS OF A SLEIGHRIDE.

Many and sweet are the songs that tell
Of those delicate sprites of wave and dell,
The elves who their moonlight revels hold
By streams that flow over sands of gold,
Or spite of the Puritan, merrily dance
Mid the groves of England and vines of France;
And the balmy breeze of Spain perfume
With the orange blossom and rose's bloom.
But the gossamer wings of these fairy bands
Wander not now to our Northern lands,
Though 'tis said, that once in these wild climes
When the feathery palms and leafy limes,
That now far down in the coalfields lie,
(Deep hid from all but the miner's eye,
And stiff as their sculptured forms would be
Carved in the blackest of ebony,)
Their full fresh foliage freely waved
O'er a silver lake their roots that laved;
They say, in that olden summer hour,
The North had ne'er felt the Frost King's power,
And sprites of these ancient groves made haunts
Who fled Old Winter like any he daunts
Till Southward in terror they swiftly fly
When his lightest of all light frosts seems nigh.

But it is not of elves who shun our air,
To sport where the sunny South is fair,
That these, my truthful rhymes, shall tell,
But of sprites who love our Northlands well.

THAT MARVELOUS SLEIGHRIDE.

'Twas a crystal eve in the Winter time :
The air as clear as the mellow chime
Of old church bells, at Christmas ringing
In hoary towers with ivy clinging, —
A simile, this, of my good old grandmother's ;
Not quite canonical, but good as some others,—
And better in this, that you know very well
What it means when you're told, "'tis as clear as
        a bell."
But similes all, are all too faint
That crystal purity to paint.
But for their likeness outlined dim
By mountains on the horizon's rim,
Of clouds the happy fickle sky
Had lost the very memory,
Earth's rimy robe of splendor lay
Sparkling with gems in the full moon's ray ;
While the oak's bare limbs, as they came between
The dazzling light of her silver sheen
And the white expanse of the outspread snow,
Cast network shadows of blue below.
The still, the clear, the frosty night
Was radiant all, and festal bright ;

Save where, within some narrowing dale,
The light grew strange, and weird and pale.
There were merry shouts; whispers low;
Tramp of steeds on crinkling snow;
Tinkling of bells; snatches of song;
All sounds that to wintry revel belong.
And they troubled, but could not break the spell
Of weird loneness within the dell.

When moonlight chastens beauty's smile
The witching hour is all the while;
And thus it chanced in a simple way
That fairies hovered about our sleigh,
As fluttering butterflies hover, and ply
Their gambols, about your path in July;
Fearless but featherly light of form
As flakes that linger after a storm
For a few more airy dances;
Fantastic imps whose goblin glee
And gay carousal were fittest to be
In a maiden's moonlit glances.

And now their circling sports they led
Where that fair light was fairest shed.
Some clasped to a glossy ringlet clung,
And frolicked, frisked and featly swung;
Some rather chose soft couch to seek
In the dimpled rose of a hooded cheek;
Or, more luxurious, slumbered well
Where muffled bosoms rose and fell;

And it wouldn't be strange if, just out of sight—
To be out of the chilly weather—
Under the furs, some mischievous sprite
Were guiding two hands to the self-same spot.
If it wasn't a sprite, 'twas : Do you know what,
When they didn't dream of coming together ?
And these were those genii quaint of the frost
Who when bright summerly tints are lost,
Adorn anew the desolate scene
With gems and silver for gold and green ;
Making the Winter fit for all mirth,
In its bracing air ; by its ruddy hearth ;
With its glare blue ice for the skater's steel ;
With its crispy snow for the cutter's keel ;
With beauty and light, and heart withal,
For ride or rout or festival ;
Fit for Christmas and New Year's to come in ;
Fit to be cozy and nice at home in ;
Fit for the country tavern ball ;
For the parson's jolly donation call,
For the social sing ; and exceedingly pat
For an hour of sparking after that ;
Fit for quilting frolics and apple bees ;
Fit for whatever revels you please :
And not a mere frightfulness, stark and blue,
A mere hole in the year for the wind to blow through.

And the fairies who made this world so fair
Were not ashamed in its mirth to share,
Like a wit his laugh who smothers.

But when their work was deftly done,
They found they had made a world of fun
For themselves as well as others.
Yet they sang a song whose varying strain,
Though it rollicked in joy had a sad refrain:
A sentimental trick, no doubt,
As Fanny sings, at the Potiphars' rout,
A lay that mentions her heart as "broke,"
Whereas that organ is much like an oak,
That is tough long after it's hollow.
However, not to digress too long,
You'll find some bits of the fairy song
In some dozen lines that follow.

SONG OF THE WINTER FAIRIES.

The merriest of brave sprites be we
Who wildly live and daintily:
For now our tiny selves we shroud
In drapery of a tempest cloud;
Now ride on the beams of a maiden's eye;
Now on a car of snowflakes fly;
And dance anon on the witching curls
That float round the necks of the Yankee girls.

Yet when November's breezes blow,
When falls the first bright broad-flaked snow,
Sadly somewhile we drop the tear
For elder daughters of the year.

While dirge-like beat the chilling waves,
We, Winter Fairies weeping bring
Spotless wreaths to deck the graves
Of Flowers that perished with the Spring.

When the marshaled storm is seen by men
To come through the pass of the Indian glen,

NOTE —In the mountainous regions of New England, the strip of
lurid sky seen above the horizon between the hills on the approach of
a storm is called "The Indian Glen."

And swift, from its mountain fastness steep,
Rank upon rank its white plumes sweep,
As they rush on the shuddering fields below,
With bladed winds and shotted snow,
In the van of the angry host ride we,
And join in its mad and martial glee.

But when upon his fading path,
The cruel storm comes down in wrath,
And, far from human voice and eye,
The traveler sinks, alone to die,
Our hands his snowy pillow smooth
Our songs his dying moments soothe ;
And through the stormy skies we bear
The accents of his last faint prayer.

The music ceased. Far up the vale
The saddened night wind seemed to wail.
But into the broad and peopled plain
The joyous revel burst again.

Again all sounds of young delight
Broke on the silence of the night;
Anew the merry song and shout
Told Echo of the madcap rout;
Anew the laugh began to ring.
But the frolic fairies all took wing;
For, all they could do being done
In the way of making love or fun,
The charms for our jollity needless more,
To the realm of Otherwhere they bore.
Seeking new fields for triumphs new
In triumph they bade our sleigh adieu.

Then the witchery that lingered there.
Was all in your eye, my blue-orbed fair!

LYRICAL PIECES.

THE GRAY OLD ELM OF PITTSFIELD PARK.

[Sung at the Humphrey Association Festival May 1, 1856.]

Tell us a tale thou gray old tree,
   A tale of thy leafy prime ;
For thine was a home in the forest free
   Ere our bold forefathers' time.
Thou sawest the wildwood all alight
   With the bale-fire's direful glare,
Where now the murkiest gloom of night
   Our household fires make fair.
Then tell us a tale, thou gray old tree,
   A tale of thy leafy prime,
Of the wild-eyed red man roaming free,
   Or our fathers' deeds sublime !

Say, when the gorgeous laurel flowers
   And sweetbriars' bloom were gay,
Did here, in the forest's fragrant hours,
   Some dusky lovers stray ?
Sadly, we know, the captive's sigh
   With thy murmuring was blent.
Oh tell of the love and courage high,
   That the captive's bondage rent !
Aye, tell us a tale, thou gray old tree,
   A tale of thy leafy prime :
Of the wild-eyed red man roaming free,
   Or our fathers' deeds sublime.

Tell us the tale how the forest fell
  And the graceful spire arose ;
And, charmed by the holy, pealing bell,
  How the valley found repose.
Our heritage here, with toil and prayer,
  Was won by the good and brave,
While over them, like a banner in air,
  They saw thy branches wave.

Then tell us a tale, thou gray old tree,
  A tale of thy leafy prime ;
Of the wild-eyed red man roaming free,
  Or our fathers' deeds sublime !

Ah, dearly we love thy wasting form,
  Thou pride of our stern old sires,
Though torn by the rage of the darting storm,
  And the lightning's scathing fires :
And dearly the sons of the mountain vale,
  Wherever their exile be,
Will thrill as they list to the song or tale,
  If it speak of their home and thee.
Then tell us a tale thou gray old tree,
  A tale of thy leafy prime :
Of the wild-eyed red man roaming free,
  Or our fathers' deeds sublime !

THE OLD ELM OF PITTSFIELD PARK.

When the first highway surveyor of the Plantation of Poontoosuc, which afterwards became the town of Pittsfield, was clearing its earliest roads of forest trees, he came upon an elm which was so beautiful that he ordered his axmen to spare it, after one of them had already inflicted two blows upon it. Think what the beauty of a tree must be to soften the heart of a highway surveyor! although this particular official, Captain Charles Goodrich, had an exceptionally large and good one. The elm was then tall, leafy in its boughs, but with its perfectly straight trunk entirely free from them to the height of fifty feet. The tree thus saved became the central figure in Pittsfield's village green ; afterwards the town's central park. In its shade occurred many of the most memorable events in the town's history. There stood the little brown meeting house in which Parson Allen preached the gospel of liberty, and the people took the boldest Revolutionary action. From under it the Pittsfield soldiery marched away to do or die in all the nation's wars. There Lafayette was received on his visit in 1825 ; and there were many similar demonstrations. There were held the first cattle shows in America of the class now universal There occurred many similar events of which it was a souvenir in the minds of all the inhabitants of the town, when they were almost all native born.

In 1841, it was one hundred and twenty-eight feet high and twenty-four in circumference. Its perfectly straight trunk was entirely bare of limbs to the height of ninety feet, but above that was a luxuriant coronal of foliage. In that year the lightning scored a ghastly wound completely down its tall, straight trunk and began to dry up its life blood. Limbs fell from it from time to time ; and twice again the lightning scathed it. Still, the little vitality which it retained was tenderly and carefully cherished by a loving community. In its palmy days strangers sang its praises and the citizens gazed upon it with pride. In its days of blight, when a few green boughs, and two or three withered and shattered limbs alone remained to crown it, the stranger still greeted it with admiration and the citizen watched it with reverent love.

On the 5th of July, 1864, it was found to be bending under its own weight and it was gently lowered from its place, literally amid the tears of stern-faced men, unused to tears. Its rings showed it to be three hundred and forty years old. Its wood was wrought into souvenirs, to which I was presumptuous enough to add the foregoing song.

KING GREYLOCK'S MOUNTAIN HEIGHT.

Written for and Sung at the Humphrey Association Festival,
Pittsfield, May 1, 1856.

With mirth and melody, ho, to-night
To scale King Greylock's mountain height.
While many a wild recess profound
Sends rattling back the echoing sound,
As we startle the sleepy forest glades
With the joyous shout of our madcap maids ;
For never a merrier band than they
Ere climbed at eve this mountain way !

CHORUS.—Then, ho, on our rude steep path, away !
            With the morrow's light on the mountain
                height ;
            We must hail the coming pomp of day !

Oh, whether its groves in sunlight lie
Or glamour moonbeams cheat the eye,
'Tis a laughing light on the mountain side,
" That owl-eyed care can never abide ;"
And his worldly chain that worldlings wear
Is loosed at the magical touch of our air,
Earth's spell is broke and the heart is free
As childhood's in its frolic glee !

CHORUS.—Then, ho, on our rude steep path, away !
　　　　With the morrow's light on the mountain
　　　　　　height ;
　　　　We must hail the coming pomp of day !

Our beacon fire this night shall glow,
A gem on the monarch mountain's brow,
Or far to our dear home valley gleam,
A new found love star's kindling beam.
Then sweeter couch ne'er wooed to rest
Then the springy boughs from the hill's green crest
For these our fragrant couch shall be,
With the star-gemmed night for canopy !

CHORUS.—Then, ho, on our rude steep path, away !
　　　　With the morrow's light on the mountain
　　　　　　height ;
　　　　We must hail the coming pomp of day !

WAHCONAH FALLS.

GREYLOCK AND WAHCONAH FALLS.

As a feature in their scenery the double peaks of
the Greylock mountain range,

> " Where look majestic forth
> From their twin thrones the Giants of the North, "

are quite as highly prized in Pittsfield and Dalton,
the southernmost towns in the upper Berkshire
valley, as they are in those of their immediate vicinity.
Greylock proper, the highest peak of the range,
and the loftiest mountain summit in Massachusetts,
rises more than thirty-five hundred feet above the
level of the sea and about twenty-five hundred
above the valley bottom in the towns named. It
affords a grand terminal for the magnificent vista
which, extending twenty miles northward, has the
Hoosac Mountains for its eastern wall and the
Taconics for its western. Naturally this mountain,
with its broad and grand overviews, is a favorite
point for excursions with the people of Pittsfield and
Dalton, and for their summer guests, as it is with
those of other towns. Those who wish to make the
most of such a trip spend the night on the mountain
top to witness the splendid spectacle of the next
morning's sunrise ; and they often—or at least often
did at the time the foregoing song was written—
kindle bonfires which can be seen twenty miles
away ; although appearing hardly larger than a star
of the first magnitude.

Pittsfield and Dalton, by virtue of their multitude
of superb and varied landscapes—aided perhaps by
the fame of some curiously interesting manufac-
tures—are constantly becoming greater favorites
with summer rest and pleasure seekers as these
attractions become more and more widely known
to the wide world beyond the mountains. And,
among the most romantic and picturesque localities
which distinguish Dalton, Wahconah Falls must be
counted; for although they are in the township of
Windsor, they are so close upon the borders of the
sister town, and are otherwise so completely identi-
fied with it, that they properly come within that
purview. They come also within the scope of our
souvenirs; for although the Lake and the Falls are
some fifteen miles apart, they—and Greylock as
well—are associated in some of my fondest memories; for it was in the same, to me delightful, years,
that, in the company of dear and congenial friends,
I learned to admire and love them all. In those
days the Falls were hardly known beyond their
immediate neighborhood, except to a few lovers
of nature's hidden nooks; her gems of the picturesque, which they held the more precious that, to
be found they must be sought. It must be con-
fessed, however, that the setting of these gems was
rather rude forty-two years ago, as the shores of
Lake Onota were.

Now the Falls are widely noted and appreciated
as among the most romantically beautiful spots in

Berkshire ; and their setting is no longer rude. Among those who in times past, most fully recognized and most highly prized their picturesque beauty was Hon. Zenas Marshall Crane, who manifested his regard by purchasing their locality, chiefly for that beauty. And his sons, Hon. Messrs. Zenas and Winthrop Murray Crane, inheriting that regard, together with the ownership, and honoring their father's memory, have so greatly improved the grounds that the many excursionists who are now attracted to the spot come away gratefully pronouncing them a park, handsome and fitting for its place.

I copy a description of the scene, which I gave some years ago :

"We soon came to the Falls—a romantic miniature cataract, just far enough removed from the highway to be sheltered from the too careless eye. Wahconah Brook, one of the larger eastern branches of the Housatonic river, here pours between perpendicular cliffs of dark gray rock a considerable volume of water, which, in two or three rapid leaps, makes a descent of seventy or eighty feet. The dark precipitous cliffs form a somber and striking vista, while the black and glossy surface of the brook affords a fine contrast with the silvery foam into which it breaks. The peculiar charm that wins for the Falls so many and so constant admirers is, however, indefinable. Perhaps it lies in the harmonious mingling of many. But be that as it may, the spot is one of those which can never fail us for a delightful hour. The swift, smooth gliding of a brook always begets pleasurable emotions, and there is rare music in the free dash of a waterfall undisturbed by the clatter of machinery."

The view of the Falls which is here presented is considered excellent by those familiar with them, except that their height is not adequately represented. To not a few excursionists the view will be a pleasing souvenir of pleasant hours.

PINOS LOQUENTES SEMPER HABEMUS.

" Lowland trees may lean to this side or to that,
though it is but a meadow breeze that bends them,
or a bank of cowslips from which their trunks lean
aslope. But let storm or avalanche do their worst;
and let the pine find only a ledge of vertical prec-
ipice to cling to, it will nevertheless grow straight.
Thrust a rod from its last shoot, down the stem; it
shall point to the center of the earth as long as the
tree stands. * * * * Other trees tufting crag
and hill, yield to the form and sway of the ground;
clothing it with soft compliance, are partly its sub-
jects, partly its flatterers, partly its comforters. But
the pine rises in serene resistance, self-contained."

RUSKIN.

All hail to the pine, to our own tasseled pine,
   The pride of our forests, the boast of our story;
A health to his tassels! still green let them shine,
   To remind the new times of the old fields of glory!
"Twas he to our fathers on Plymouth's bleak shore,
The first shelter gave and the first welcome bore.
Then a health to thy tassels, our own native pine;
A halo of glory above us they shine!

All hail to the pine on our banner that waved
   Ere plumed was our eagle or starry flags floated!
On field and on fortress where tyrants were braved
   The pine on that banner the victor denoted.

It marched in the van where our minutemen met ;
Its folds with the blood of our Warren were wet :
Grand voices of story heroic are thine,
And we thrill to thy murmurs proud. eloquent pine·

All hail to the pine, fadeless type of the true !
    The changeless in beauty, unbending, undaunted.
The banner of green to the May breeze he threw,
    In the gales of December, as boldly are flaunted.
He dares the fierce blast when the tempest sweeps by,
Nor faints in the glare from the hot summer sky.
Grand poet, pure teacher, High Priest of Truth's
        shrine,
Thou art evermore with us. thrice eloquent pine !

THANKSGIVING MORNING SONG.

Air, Auld Lang Syne.

We meet again around the hearth
    Where oft we used to come ;
We've gathered from the wilds of Earth
    To this our father's home.

CHORUS.—We'll wake again the joys of old,
        The joys of old so dear ;
    And memory with her chain of gold,
        Shall closer bind us here !

The dust and clouds of toil and care
The world hath o'er us flung,
Shall vanish in the pure, clear air
We breathed when we were young.

Chorus.—We'll wake again, etc.

The noisy clang of jarring throngs
Shall vex our ear no more
Nor break upon the peaceful songs
We loved and sang of yore!

Chorus.—We'll wake again, etc.

Bring back the sports of old that came
With each Thanksgiving's glee:
No child shall join in childhood's game
More light of heart than we.

Chorus.—We'll wake again, etc.

We've left the haunts of common mirth,
We've gathered, one and all,
To hold around our father's hearth,
Our fathers' festival.

Chorus.—We'll wake again the joys of old,
The joys of old so dear;
And memory with her chains of gold,
Anew shall bind us here!

THANKSGIVING EVENING SONG.

We have met again in our father's home,
Round the hearth where we used of old to come.
We have prayed in the church where of old we-
      prayed ;
Our steps have been where of old they strayed :
We have felt the breeze that was wont to play
With our youthful locks on Thanksgiving Day.
We have greeted each scene we loved to greet ;
We have sat at the board where we used to meet :
Oh, why should a shadow be o'er us cast,
As you sing to-night, glad songs of the past ?

We meet again but we meet not all
Who were wont to come at our father's call.
We have knelt where they prayed, but still and cold
Are the hearts whose glow warmed ours of old.
We have roamed each haunt where we loved to rove ;
By the rippling brook, in the whispering grove :
The wood and the streamlet murmured still
As when, like glad music, their sounds could thrill :
But we missed the silvery laugh that gave
Their tone of joy to the wood and the wave.

No ; we meet in our home : but not as of yore.
It hath lost a charm to be found no more :
From our festal wreath the rose is gone,
The fairest star from our sky of morn,

From our choral band the sweetest voice.
When your songs in the gladness of youth rejoice,
An unvoiced burden comes, deep and clear,
To our inmost souls : "They are not here !"
It is thus that a shadow is o'er us cast,
While you sing to-night glad songs of the past.

A CHRISTMAS CAROL.

Hark to the bells! the Christmas bells,
    Come again with their olden voices!
The air rebounds to the joyous sounds
    And the waking world rejoices!
The crystal chimes! the merry chimes!
    On Christmas day at morning.
They welcome the blaze of the festal rays
    That, bright, in the east are dawning.

Now joy to earth and chainless mirth;
    All the revels of yore repeating!
Warm hands be pressed, and your neighbor blessed
    With the old and kindly greeting!
And peal the chimes, the olden chimes
    Of Christmas day at morning.
And sing the songs, the olden songs,
    That hailed its festal dawning!

Bring the brighter sheen of our native green,
    If you lack the glossy holly;
To deck the hearth for a sign of mirth,—
    And, perchance, of harmless folly,
But bring us these, if naught but these,
    Warm hearts with kindness glowing,
And sunny eyes where laughter lies
    And lovelight overflowing!

ODE FOR INDEPENDENCE DAY.

Hark! a nation's shouts ascend!
Hark a myriad voices blend!
From your thrones of glory bend,
    Sires of Liberty!

From each proud empurpled field
Where your blood our freedom sealed,
Spirit tongues to-day have pealed
    Freedom's Jubilee!

Where the smoke of battle curled,
Where the bolt of death was hurled
Ye our starry flag unfurled,
    Floating o'er the free!

In the dark and trying time,
Arming for your native clime,
Ye stood in native might sublime.
    Undauntedly!

Flashing sword and burning word,
By foemen felt, by freemen heard,
Plumed our country's banner bird
    Right gallantly!

Patriot sires of glory's days,
While the world resounds your praise,
Hear the songs your children raise.
    Songs of Liberty!

REAPERS' HYMN.

Now joy for the land
  With garnered fruits o'erflowing,
Of plains that teem with golden grains,—
  Our own, our native land ;
And be His grateful praises pealed
Who bade the earth her increase yield,
And gave each fertile field !
      Oh, praise, praise His hand !

Your praise, brothers, bring
  For Autumn's glowing treasures,
For golden rays of summer days
  And showers of the spring.
We're bearing home the glorious spoil
We've gathered from our own free soil,
We've won by honest toil :
      Right joyfully sing !

With joy, reapers, sing ;
  No tyrant arm is o'er us.
The fields we've sown were all our own ;
  Oh, gratefully sing !
And when we take their fruit and grain,
Our souls are free from robber stain.
With heart and voice again,
Then praise, brothers, bring !

A NORTHLAND SONG.

Let weaklings fly to a Southern sky
   When our own gleams somewhat coldly;
We'll have our bout with the storm king out,
   And face his legions boldly.
'Tis a joyous time when the glittering rime
   O'er all our landscape gloweth;
And our warm blood thrills on the Boreal hills
   When the quickening north wind bloweth.

Old Winter came our lives to tame.
   And rule with a tyrant's rigor;
But we fought him long till our hearts grew strong
   As we made our own his vigor!
We've laughed at his rage from youth to age,
   And joyed in his mad disporting:
The blasts of his pride with glee defied:
   A tiff with his wild gales courting.

On his roughest day, we trudged our way
   To the hut of birch-sped learning,
On our snow-piled path from his tempest's wrath
   In his fiercest mood ne'er turning.
His nipping nights, our young delights
   Made soft with their sweet compelling;
And our jangled bells to his hills and dells,
   Rang out, our victory telling!

In his lordliest hour, we braved his power,
  When his snows the hilltops crested :
Shall we turn and flee—no, no! not we !—
  From the blasts we so oft have breasted ?
Let weaklings fly to a Southern sky
  When our own gleams somewhat coldly ;
We'll have our bout with the storm king out
  And face his legions boldly !

THE LOGGER'S SONG.

  Up, brothers, join our march to-night.
  The crinkling snow is sparkling bright ;
  The ringing echoes far prolong
  The chorus of our wild road song,
  And the startled deer from his covert springs.
  As our shout through the forest arches rings,
  And off to his mountain fastness hies.
  Where silver-white Katahdin lies
    Aglow with the full moon's light !

CHORUS.—Come away then, ye stalwart pack,
      To the forest deep, where the wild deer leap,
      And the moose, o'er our frozen track !

STARTING LARGE.

Up, comrades; leave your dull fireside!
Through cloudless skies the moonbeams glide;
Your Northern blood will leap, I ween,
Where cuts the night air clear and keen,
While the golden stars with a softer beam
Through the frozen mist of the river gleam,
And, garlanded with radiant snow,
The pines their tasseled branches throw
 Far over our pathway wild.

CHORUS.—Come, away then, ye stalwart pack,
  To the forest deep where the wild deer leap.
  And the moose, o'er our frozen track!

One gentle thought to some we leave
Who'll miss our step this fall of eve;
For maiden thoughts full oft will stray
From festal rooms to the woods away:
And we—we will chime with the wintry blast
As he whistles our forest dwelling past,
A song to tell the rushing storm
That the Logger's heart beats true and warm
 For the fair and far away.

CHORUS.—Then up and away, ye stalwart pack,
  To the forest deep, where the wild deer leap,
  And the moose, o'er our frozen track!

A SONG OF MAY.

Air, "Love Not."

Blow on, blow on,
Ye balmy winds of Spring,
  As o'er my grateful cheek but now ye strayed ;
What dreamy bliss your soft caresses bring ;
  Gaily around me thus of old ye played.
      Blow on, blow on.

Beam out, beam out,
Thou laughing sun of May ;
  Oh, pour your brightest beams on youthful love :
Buoyant of old beneath a sky as gay,
  Of hope and joy my web of life I wove.
      Beam out, beam out.

Flow on, flow on,
Thou silver-leaping rill ;
  To yon fair grove where chants the tuneful bird ;
Not one bright joy hath lost the power to thrill
  With which my glad young heart of old was stirred.
      Flow on, flow on.

THE SACHEM'S DAUGHTER.

Bright as the foam on Casco's water
    Ere it played round the white man's prow,
Was the laughing eye of the Sachem's daughter,
    So cold and rayless now.
Oh, what was the spell in the stranger's glances
    That hath blighted our fairest flower;
For she joins no more our greenwood dances,
    Nor smiles the livelong hour.

Once on the breeze Kenduska's laughter
    Through the forest arches rung,
While the woodland sprites sent echoes after,
    And wild flowers o'er her flung.
But when the spray in the moonlight glistened,
    And she stood by the murmuring shore,
To the stranger's song our wild bird listened,
    And sings her own no more.

She stood on the sad, lone beach, beholding
    The sea-mist fly from the morn's array,
When the stranger's ship, white wings unfolding,
    Sped swiftly from our bay.
Oh, say, when afar in the blue it vanished,
    Did it carry our sister's light?
For the star-beams from her eye are banished;
    They do not cheer her night.

THE PRETTY ROSALIE.

Where the lights so cheerily
  O'er youth and beauty glow,
There with pretty Rosalie
  The moments sparkling flow.
With a Tra, la, la, la, la, la, la !
  But my pretty Rosalie,
At home I'd like to know,
  So cheery would you be,
When, pit-pat, pit-pat raindrops go ?
  Heigho ! Would you though,
With your Tra, la, la, la, la, la, la !

Where the music merrily
  In joyous chorus rings.
There the pretty Rosalie
  Enchanteth while she sings,
Tra, la, la, la, la, la, la !
  But, my pretty Rosalie,
At home I'd like to know,
  So would you sing that strain,
Married should we be,
  When pit-pat raindrops go ?
Pit-pat choruseth the rain ;
  Not Tra, la, la, la, la, la, la !

SERENADE.

All is still; no voices wake;
  On all the charméd air,
No murmurs break;
  No song nor sound is there;
Save but where
  Peals our lone lay,
O lady fair, to thee,
  While the winds stay their wild way,
To listen silently.

Calm and clear, looks down the while
Fond night with tender eyes.
  Her sweetest smile
On all around us lies—
  Softly lies.
List now our lay,
  O lady fair, to thee,
While the winds stay their wild way
  To harken breathlessly.

Summer nights are fair, but fleet.
  Soon comes the morn!
With smile more sweet,
  The smiling scene adorn,
Ere it be gone;
  And list our lay,
O, lady fair, to thee,
  While the winds stay their wild way
To harken silently!

NOT THROUGH GLORY'S MYRTLE ARCHES.

Not through glory's myrtle arches,
Not with proud triumphal marches,
    Shall we reach our Heavenly home :
But through paths oft wild and dreary,
And with footsteps worn and weary,
    To the Rest of God we come.

Not by deeds that live in story,—
Deeds that win a martyr's glory,
    Can our Heavenly crown be won :
But by faith devout and holy,
By a spirit meek and lowly,
    When our greatest work is done.

By the prayer in secret glowing,
By the tear in secret flowing,
    Must our Heavenward race be won :
By Calvary's rugged path ascending,
On the cross alone depending,
    When our purest work is done.

EVENING HYMN.

The gorgeous day on sunny wing
  Hath sped his weary flight,
And stars in milder glory bring
  The welcome hours of night:
To Thee, our guide, our guard by day,
  Its peaceful close be given.
O, thou who cheered our toilsome way,
  Receive our praise at even.

For strength when sultry noontide glowed,
  For love that crowns the eve;
For every good Thou hast bestowed,
  Our grateful praise receive.
Thou wast our guide, our guard by day;
  To Thee its close be given.
O Thou who cheered our toilsome way,
  Receive our praise at even.

And when our life's brief day declines,
  So calmly fade its light,
While brighter, and yet brighter shines
  Faith's star upon the night.—
O, guard us through life's weary day,
  Guide to its peaceful even;
And when its last gleam fades away,
  Receive our praise in Heaven.

OUR WARRIOR WORLD.

Here's speed to the World, our own round World,
　As he rolls through the realms of space !
'Gainst Time and his steeds, on his way he speeds,
　Nor tires in the breathless race.
But as on he hies, from more he flies
　Than his twin-born rival, Time,
For there follow still, foul forms and ill,--
　Dire Woes and their father, Crime.
Then pray for the World, our own swift World,
　As he rolls through the realms of space ;
'Gainst Woe and Crime, with strength sublime,
　He speeds on his fearful race.

Here's strength to the World, our own brave World,
　For he battles as he flies !
He hath battled long, and many a wrong
　About his pathway dies ;
Earth's giant woes, in mortal throes,
　With wounds are writhing sore ;
But he girds his might for the race and fight
　Till the battle shall be o'er.
Then pray for the World, our own brave World,
　As he rolls through the realms of space ;
'Gainst Woe and Crime, in strength sublime,
　He speeds to the fight and race.

Here's joy to the World, our glad, strong World,
    As he sweeps on his viewless wings!
With the Thunder's voice his hills rejoice,
    And the Storm his triumph sings.
But his gladdest strain hath a bold refrain,
    With a shrill alarum tone :
For he battles still the hosts of Ill
    Till the Right shall reign alone.
Then pray for the World, our Warrior World,
    That he conquer to the end,
When the choral spheres, for mortal ears,
    Again their songs shall blend.

THE FAIRIES OF THE HILLS.

[A cantata, written for a *Soirée Musicale* of the Maplewood
Young Ladies' Institute, Pittsfield, February 7, 1856. Music
by James L. Ensign.]

SOLO,—*First Fairy.*

> Right joyous sprites, and blithe, be we,
> Who gaily live and daintily;
> For our home is the green old mountain vale
> Afar from the city's mournful wail,
> And the task the Master gives us there
> Is to render all things bright and fair.

Full Chorus of Fairies.

> And a dainty life we live alway
> In the darkling wood and the sparkling ray.

First Semi Chorus.

> We build the woodland arches fair,
> We hang the leaflet curtains there.

Second Semi Chorus.

> We lay the carpet of velvet green,
> We polish the mirrored lake, serene.

First Semi Chorus.

> We paint the flowers of varied hue.

Second Semi Chorus.

> We tint the sky with its deepest blue.

First Semi Chorus.
    We silver the cloud.

Second Semi Chorus.
    We gem the foam.

The Two Semi Choruses.
    And thus we build us a fairy home !

Full Chorus.
    Aye, and a dainty life, etc.

SOLO,—*Second Fairy.*
    And glad alway is our dainty life,
    With a myriad rarest pleasures rife.
    For our music, we list to rill or bird,
    Or laughter from gypsying childhood heard ;
    Or a softer voice may thrill the grove—
    For our fairy home is the bower of love.

Third and Fourth Fairies.
    Thus we live till the emerald hues we've laid
    On Summer leaves begin to fade ;
    Then, when along the Western skies,
    Day like the changeful dolphin dies,
    We steal the tints of the gorgeous eves
    To hide the blight on the forest leaves,
    Till anew the Autumn hillsides glow
    With a splendor Summer woods ne'er know.

Semi Chorus.
    That Summer woods ne'er know.

Full Chorus.

And a dainty life we live alway
In the darkling wood and the sparkling ray.

First Semi Chorus.

We crimson the maple, we gild the beech;
Each leaf some strange bright hue we teach.

Second Semi Chorus.

The valley had never a fairer scene,
The streamlet had never a brighter sheen.

First Semi Chorus.

But fairest splendor must fade and die,

Second Semi Chorus.

Then summon our chariot birds and fly!

First Semi Chorus.

The Summer is past.

Second Semi Chorus.

The storms will come.

The Two Semi Choruses.

Then hie away from our fairy home!
Farewell! Farewell! Farewell! Farewell!

Full Chorus.

Farewell to the bowers where we lay
In the laughing leafy Summer day.
               Farewell! Farewell!

CHILDREN'S SONGS.

Forty-two years ago I wrote a number of songs for "The Wreath of School Songs;" a little music book published at Boston, which had a remarkably wide use in Maine, Massachusetts, and probably other states. I copy here four of the songs; wondering whether they will be souvenirs of their schooldays to any of the many thousands who sang them in their childhood. If not, it may be that forty-two years hence, when this book shall have been forgotten by almost every other reader, they may be souvenirs to my little Walter and Bessie, of the uncle who was the playmate of their infancy, before they could read his verses; or even tease him for stories.

LONG, LONG AGO.

Air, "Long Ago."

Tell me the tale of the friends that you loved
     Long, long ago.
Tell me of those by whose side you have roved
     Long, long ago.
Say were your schoolmates as blithe and as gay,
Joyous as those I have been with to-day?
Who were the children you met in your play.
     Long, long ago?

What were the pleasures you joyed in at home,
Long, long ago?
What were the meadows enticed you to roam,
Long, long ago?
Mother, sweet mother, why starteth that tear?
Tell me the tales you delighted to hear
Told by the friends that to you were so dear,
Long, long ago.

CHILDHOOD'S HOME.

Around the blazing hearth of home,
Night and day,
With happy hearts we love to come,
While kindly smiles about us play :
Night and day.
Sweet smiles about us play !

While sweeps the wintry blast around,
Cold and drear,
We love to hear the stormy sound,
While cheerful fire is glowing near :
Bright and clear.
The fire is glowing near !

Our cheerful songs we love to sing
Around the hearth.
We love to make our voices ring
With fairy tales and words of mirth, —
Around the hearth,
With light and airy mirth !

VACATION SONG.

Come out! The sunlight calls to rove,
　And breathe the balmy air;
Come, wander through the leafy grove,
　And by the streamlet fair.

We come on sunny meads to lie,
　And sing a merry strain:
And thus vacation moments fly,
　Till schooltime comes again.

Come out awhile, my schoolmates all,
　From thought and study free:
Come out! Obey my merry call,
　To careless, frolic glee!

No wonder that we dearly love
　Vacation's happy hours,
When free we wander through the grove,
　And pluck the fragrant flowers.

GOD IS THERE.

When o'er Earth is breaking
　Rosy light and fair,
Morn afar proclaimeth
　Sweetly "God is there."

When the Spring is wreathing
  Flowers rich and rare,
On each leaf is written
  " Nature's God is there."

When the storm is raging
  Through the midnight air,
In mighty tones its thunder
  Tells us " God is there."

All the wide world gives us,
  Rich, or grand, or fair,
Everywhere bears graven,
  " God, our God, is there."

TRANSLATIONS

FROM THE GERMAN.

THE VOYAGERS.

From the German of Albert Knapp.

He who on the broad Atlantic,
   Launches from his native strand
Finds no draught to quench his thirsting
   Save that he bears from land.

Boundless waters may surround him,
   Countless billows round him play.
But not all of that salt ocean
   Can the wanderer's thirsting stay.

Child of man, so goest thou voyaging
   On the wide world's thronging waves,
And not all its whirl of waters
   Gives the draught thy bosom craves.

Fullest overflow of pleasure
   Is with longing sense alloyed :
All its billows, rising, sinking,
   Leave the soul unstayed and void.

Thou hast need of other water
   Than the stormy world-sea knows :
Pure as dews when morn or evening
   In the rosy heaven glows.

Craves thy soul a living water
  To the springs of Earth unknown :
Welling from the Heavenly fountains
  Fast beside the Eternal Throne.

Go out upon life's bitter ocean,
  But that purer water take.
Ask it of thy gracious Saviour,
  Who will all thy thirsting slake.

Who from Him the cup receiveth
  Drinks and thirsteth never more
Till he reach the Heavenly haven
  On the everlasting shore.

THE LAST SHADOW.

From the German of Albert Knapp.

Where, in the hush'd and curtain'd room,
  The good old man was lying,
A gloom upon the living fell,
  But radiance on the dying.

For fourscore years this checker'd earth,
  Of sun and shade, he trod.
And walked—alike in firm-paced youth
  And tottering age—with God.

But when low, sobbing voices asked :
　" How fares it with thee, now ? "
Light not of earth, while thus he spake,
　Illumed his wrinkled brow :

" My soul, like an eagle, seeks the skies,
　On the morning's rosy breath—
Before but the rising sun of Life,
　Behind but the Shadow—Death ! "

FAIR CEDAR TREE.

Fair cedar tree how evergreen,
　How changeless are thy leaflets !
We greet thy shade in Summer's glow,
And, beautiful mid Winter's snow,
　We turn to thee, fair cedar tree
And bless thy changeless leaflets.

Oh teach to man thy constant truth ;
　Make firm his faithless bosom,
Who swears to stand forever true
When winds are fair and skies are blue ;
　But flies his trusting brother's side,
His sorest need unaided.

The nightingale, false nightingale,
  To fickle man has taught her lesson.
Through Summer eves she breathes delights,
But fails the fall of Winter nights.
  The nightingale, false nightingale,
Change with the times has taught him.

The mountain brook is rightly mankind's mirror :
  Is rightly mankind's mirror.
It mocks the swain through April showers.
But fails the sultry Summer hours ;
  The mountain brook, false mountain brook,
Is rightly mankind's mirror.

But cedar tree, fair cedar tree,
  Still changeless are thy leaflets.
We greet thy shade in Summer's glow,
And beautiful mid Winter's snow.
  We turn to thee, dear cedar tree,
And bless thy changeless leaflets.

KORNER'S BATTLE HYMN.

[Charles Theodore Körner was born at Dresden in 1791. Before he was twenty-two years old, he won a fair, although not very great, reputation as a poet. In 1813 began the war for the redemption of Germany from the tyranny of Napoleon and his invading armies. Then young Körner, abandoning the fairest prospects for success and happiness in civil life, took up the sword and the pen in behalf of his country's freedom. In a few impassioned weeks,—besides eloquent prose in support of the same holy cause—he wrote fervid, patriotic, martial poetry which seems to me to excel in every respect any verse of the same class in any language—hardly excepting La Marseillaise or "Scots, wha hae wi' Wallace bled." Early in his military service he was severely wounded; but, returning to the field, he fell in battle, August 26, 1813. His sister died of grief for his loss, surviving him only long enough to paint his portrait from memory—a touching story which afforded Mrs. Hemans a theme for her beautiful poem, "Körner and his Sister," of which the following is the first stanza :

"Green wave the oak forever o'er thy rest,
   Thou that beneath its crowning foliage sleepest,
And in the stillness of thy country's breast,
   Thy place of memory like an altar keepest.

Brightly thy spirit o'er her hills was poured,
    Thou of the Lyre and the Sword."

The following tender adieu is the closing verse
of the same poem.

" Have ye not met ere now? So let those trust
  That meet for moments, but to part for years,—
That weep,watch, pray, to hold back dust from dust.—
  That love where love is but a fount of tears.
Brother, sweet sister, peace around ye dwell :
    Lyre, sword and flower, farewell !"

THE BATTLE HYMN.

Shortly before his death Körner wrote the Battle Hymn,
which is translated below.

    Father, on Thee I call !
Darkly the clouds of the battle surround me ;
Fiercely the sword of the foe flashes round me ;
  God of the battle, on Thee I call.
    Father, be Thou my guide !

    Father, be Thou my guide ;
Lead me to death, or to victory lead me ;
Lead where the cause of my country may need me ;
  Lord, where Thou wilt, but be Thou my guide.
    Father, Thy power, I own !

Father. Thy power, I own!
As in the fall of the leaves of the forest,
So when we yield to the war's iron tempest,
　　Fountain of glory. Thy power, I own.
　　　Father, oh, bless Thy son!

　　Father, oh, bless Thy son!
Calmly my life to Thy hand I deliver:
Be Thou its guardian, as Thou wast its giver.
　　Living or dying, yet bless Thy son!
　　　Father, for this I pray!

　　Father, to Thee I pray:
'Tis for no treasures of Earth we're contending;
Holiest of rights, with the sword, we're defending.
　　Victor or vanquished, to Thee I pray:
　　　Battling, I dare to pray!

THE LILIES OF THE MUMMEL SEE.

Mummel See is lone and drear,
　　Yet there are sweetest lilies blooming;
And, bending low, their kiss they yield,
　　The wanton breeze of morn perfuming:
But when the night on Earth comes down
And its fair queen assumes her crown,
From the dark wave each flower uprises,
Like youthful maids in festal guises.

The winds that whistle through the grove,
   Give fitting music for their dances,
While on the shore each lily maid
   Through mazy circles deftly glances.
Their graceful forms, how slight! how frail!
How white their robes! their cheeks how pale!
Till the warm dance at length discloses
Among the lilies, blended roses!

Now howls the wind; now rolls the storm,
   Through gloomy forests fiercely sweeping;
The moon in clouds has hid her form,
   And murkier shades o'er Earth are creeping.
Still, up and down, the dance goes round,
To the tempest-tune, on the rough wet ground;
While the foam on the lake-wave whiter flashes
As its crest on the shore it higher dashes.

An arm from out the lake is raised.
   A giant hand, and clenched, outthrowing:
A dripping head with sedges crowned,
   And a white beard, long and flowing.
Then a voice is heard, with a thunder tone,
That echoes afar through the mountains lone:
" Back, vagrant lilies, to your native waters!
Back to your homes, unduteous daughters!"

The dance is stilled; the maids grow wan;
   'Tis sad to hear their fitful shrieking:
"Our father calls! Ha! morning air!
   Back then; our cheerless waters seeking."—

The silver mists from out the valley rise,
And morning painteth gay the Eastern skies;
Again the lilies to the winds are swaying,
Their pale meek heads upon the waters laying.

NOTE.—Mummel See—Literally, "The Dismal or Gloomy
Lake." I do not know who is the author of this ballad. I
found it many years ago on a loose leaf, apparently from some
German magazine, flying before the wind on Boston Common.
I thought it beautiful, but did not translate it on that account;
but because it reminded me of Melville (since called Morewood)
Lake, in the Broadhall grounds in Pittsfield. That romantic
little sheet of water is far enough from being gloomy, dismal or
lone: but it has an abundance of lilies on its surface, so
attractive that the poet Longfellow, as he tells us in his diary,
when a guest at Broadhall, was tempted to gather some of
them for his children, at some considerable risk of his life: the
only boat at hand being in a most dangerously dilapidated
condition. This profusion of water lilies led the ladies of
Broadhall to fancifully christen their pretty lakelet, "The
Lily Bowl;" and it is so designated on one map. There are
some pleasing legends, both historic and mythical, about the
Lily Bowl; but I have not heard that its lilies are in the habit
of leaving their comfortable beds, where to mortal view, they
seem to sleep very soundly, to "come out," like Bowery girls,
to "dance by the light of the moon." Graceful dances on the
lake shore are too frequent by daylight for it to need, even in
fancy, such moonlit visitations; and, moreover, the lilies of the
"Lily Bowl" are naturally not so restless as their less happy
kindred of the Mummel See.

IVAN'S CROSS.

From the German of Albert Knapp.

On the Kremlin's loftiest dome stood a cross of
  giant height,
Like another sun in heaven, shedding round a golden
  light ;
Telling there the awe-struck gazer, "Great Russia
  too relied
In the fullness of her power, on a Saviour
  crucified !"

But when Murat's cuirassiers thundered over Mos-
  cow's streets,
And the Emperor held his court in the Kremlin's
  holy seats,
Napoleon looked up where the Cross majestic shone,
Looking down in silent grandeur on his transient,
  trembling throne.

He had torn from Europe's capitals all that proudest
  was in art,
To deck Paris with such glory as bold robbery can
  impart,
And he swore to sunny France a trophied spoil to
  bear,
The Cross that rose so grandly through the crystal
  northern air !

" Take it down and bear it with us," then the victor
    Emperor cries,
" On our distant Notre Dame a memento it shall
    rise,
Telling to our children's children what their bold
    forefathers braved,
When the Frenchman's Eagle-banner over conquered
    Moscow waved."

Engineers then climbing, crowding, reached the
    Cross that rose so calm :
Struck and wrenched, and downward thrust it, iron
    tool and strong-nerved arm,
Till the noble victim fell, groaning, from its throned
    height,
As the soaring eagle falls, death-struck in his up-
    ward flight.

Yet not quietly they have it ! How the crowding
    ravens flutter !
Hov'ring round it, vengeful, threat'ning cries they
    utter ;
Hear them shrieking, moaning, groaning, for their
    tearful, woeful loss ;
Say they in their heart-sick mourning—" Spare our
    dear old friendly Cross ! "

Not the sapper's gleaming axes can the birds of
    omen scare,
From where, 'twixt spoil and spoiler, their threat-
    'ning flight they dare ;

Till the Emperor asks in wonder, " Do the birds
    lament the Cross ? "
" Aye, Sire ; and you may rue its gain more than
    we now rue its loss ! "

*   *   *   *   *

When on many a field of horror, shrouded in the
    whirling snows,
Soon that host of victors stiff'ning on the plains of
    Russia froze ;
Then on every marble victim, and on every snowy
    shroud,
Crowds of ravens, hoarsely shrieking, croaked their
    vengeful glee aloud.

EVENING AMONG THE MOUNTAINS.

When the stars in golden beauty
    Through the fading twilight gleam,
And the dew-gemmed flowerets glisten
    In the moonlight's silver beam, —
Then a sense of love and longing
    O'er my soul will softly come
And my eye look through its tear-drops
    To its far-off spirit home.

Rest unbroken, holy silence
　　Reign o'er all around me here.
Silently the ghost-like vapors
　　White and high their forms uprear :
Phantasy with kindly visions
　　Soothes the lonely heart of woe,
In the mountain mist restoring
　　Love-lost forms of long ago.

Then the vanished dreams of childhood
　　Bright and fair come back again ;
Joy descends from Heaven around me,
　　Free from taint of earthly pain.
Wondrous music sweetly cheers me ;
　　Fairest flowers their perfume shed.
Eager beats the heart to clasp them ;
　　But the phantom joys have fled.

Stormy clouds come thronging darkly ;
　　One by one the stars are lost,
And I see the pale moon only,
　　In the heavens tempest tost.—
Ah, 'tis thus our early dream-life
　　Fades when life with tumult teems :
And we seek—how long, how vainly—
　　Phantom joys of life's young dreams.

LATIN

TRANSLATION.

DULCE DOMUM—SWEET HOME.

EXPLANATORY.—Some fifty years ago I copied into my scrapbook, from " *The Euterpiad*," an excellent musical and literary magazine then published in New York, the Latin student-song printed below. The magazine stated that it had been sung from time immemorial by the students of some English college or at a school like Eton, (I now forget which) as they were about to start homeward at the beginning of vacation. At intervals for about half a century I have been on the point of attempting a translation ; but the task of putting a Latin song into lyrical and rhymed English, is by no means so attractive a pastime as doing the same by a German ballad. So I procrastinated in this, as in matters of more moment. But the other day it occurred to me that if there are any dropped stitches in any life work of mine that I intend ever to take up, it is time to be about it ; and this translation seemed worth the making, as a souvenir of college days, if no more ; and I therefore set about it. Latin retired to a back chamber of one's brain for fifty years, with few and brief airings, gets rather stiff in the joints ; but I have managed to make mine hobble, after a fashion, for this short jaunt. " Daulius advena " in the fourth stanza, however, staggered me for a while. Who could this Daulian wanderer be ? But one

sleepless night, the door of that brain's backroom
got ajar, as it will in such hours, and the answer
popped out.   It is told in a familiar, but horrible,
Greek fable that Philomela, for her unwitting part
in some shocking sins, was, as a mild punishment,
transformed into a nightingale and condemned to
wail her penitence through Summer nights for all
time.   The scene of this tragic tale is laid in the
very old Grecian city of Daulius and the nightingale
was, therefore, sometimes called "The Daulian
Bird."   But why "wanderer"? That was for the
artistic purpose of the song writer, who supposes
the nightingale, after wandering about all night with
her plaintive serenade, to be returning to her nest at
daybreak, as the students, after the weary toils of
term-time, were about to hasten home for vacation.
Thus "Daulius advena" is clearly a synonym—
although a far-fetched, and perhaps pedantic, one
—for a wandering nightingale.   This and other
parts of the song show that it was intended to be
sung in the early morning while the students were
waiting for the coaches that were to convey them to
their homes.   And we can almost see and hear
those old college boys or, rather, those college boys
of the olden time, as they sing, shout and stamp
their impatience.   The song forcibly expresses their
appreciation of, and eagerness for, the pleasures of
"Sweet Home" in many of its lines; but uniquely
by its manifold reiteration of the fond words in its
remarkably redundant chorus.

The Latin of the song may not be of Horatian purity, and the translation may be imperfect. I therefore print them together; so that any young Latin scholar may better them if he thinks it worth the trouble.

The song and its story are both interesting in themselves; but my attention was first drawn to them by the coincidence of the refrain with that of Howard Payne's world-famous lyric, whose simple melody and naturalness have enabled millions to give voice to that love of home which dwells in all unseared hearts, and, like every genuine sentiment, seeks expression in song. Whether there was any connection beyond mere accidental coincidence between the two refrains is a matter of curious conjecture only; not at all affecting the originality of the later tribute to home, whose history is as follows:

In the year 1823, Miss M. Tree was playing as the prima donna at a London theatre in Payne's opera, "The Maid of Milan." The opera had a long run, and Miss Tree, fearing that the public would weary of its frequent repetition, requested the author to enliven it by introducing a new song. He furnished "Sweet Home;" and what has since come of it all the world knows. Being in England, he may have heard of the students' Latin *Dulce Domum;* but the expression "Sweet Home" is so natural that he may have heard it from any, indeed from many, lips. In either case it merely furnished him a theme upon which he wrought out an entirely independent melody.   It is still more probable that the theme, as well as his treatment of it, was inspired by his own homesickness in that loneliest of dwelling-places for the stranger, a great metropolis.

This explanation—so far as it relates to the later song of Sweet Home—may seem superfluous.   I make it lest some over-jealous hypercritic should fancy that I am silly enough to think that the revival of the old student home-song will impugn the originality of an American melody that was never known until the author's actress-friend introduced it in her play ; but which has since, either in its words or the instrumental music that represents them, been more often heard than any other, unless it may be, such national airs as "God Save the Queen" in England and the "Star Spangled Banner" in America.

Pittsfield, February 4, 1895.

DULCE DOMUM.

Concinnimus, O Sodales !
Eja ! quid silemus ?
  Nobile canticum !
  Dulce melos, domum !
Dulce domum, resonemus.

CHORUS.—Domum, domum, dulce domum !
    Domum, domum, dulce domum !
    Dulce, dulce domum !
    Dulce domum, resonemus !

Appropinquat ecce felix
  Hora gaudiorum,
Post grave tedium,
Advenit omnium
Meta petita laborum !

CHORUS.—Domum, domum, dulce domum !
    Domum, domum, dulce domum !
    Dulce, dulce domum !
    Dulce domum, resonemus !

Musa, libros mitte, fessa ;
Mitte pensa dura :
Mitte negotium !
Jam datur otium,
Ite mea metita cura !

CHORUS.—Domum, domum, dulce domum !
    Domum, domum, dulce domum !
    Dulce, dulce domum !
    Dulce domum, resonemus !

Ridet annus ! prata rident !
Nosque rideamus.
  Jam repetit domum
  Daulius advena !
Nosque, domum repetemus !

CHORUS.—Domum, domum, dulce domum !
    Domum, domum, dulce domum !
    Dulce, dulce domum !
    Dulce domum, resonemus !

Heus! rogare fer caballos!
Eja! nunc eamus;
Limen amabile,
Matres et oscula,
Suaviter et repetemus;

CHORUS.—Domum, domum, dulce domum!
Domum, domum, dulce domum!
Dulce, dulce domum,
Dulce domum, resonemus!

Concinnimus ad Penates!
Vox et audiatur!
Phosphore! quid jubar
Segnius emicans
Gaudia nostra moratur?

CHORUS.—Domum, domum, dulce domum!
Domum, domum, dulce domum!
Dulce, dulce domum!
Dulce domum, resonemus!

SWEET HOME.

Classmates in choral song join we!
How can we silent be?
'Tis a noble strain;
Sweet melody: Home!
Sweet home, we sing again!

CHORUS.—Home, home, sweet home!
    Home, home, sweet home!
    Sweet, sweet home!
    Sweet home, we shout again!

 Lo, the happy hours draw nigh, boys;
 The task-free time of joys!
  Past its dragging tedium,
 The long-sought end hath come.
 Of all our labors tiresome!

CHORUS.—Home, home, sweet home!
    Home, home, sweet home!
    Sweet, sweet home!
    Sweet home, we shout again!

 Weary muse, put books away:
 Studious thought no longer stay!
 Duties give place to play!
 Now rest is given the heart,
 You, too, my meted tasks, depart!

CHORUS.—Home, home, sweet home!
    Home, home, sweet home!
    Sweet, sweet home!
    Sweet home, we shout again!

 Now smiles the sky; the meadows smile;
 And we will gladsome be the while!
 Ceasing the night hours to beguile,

The wandering nightingale flies home;
And we to ours will fleetly come!

CHORUS.—Home, home, sweet home!
Home, home, sweet home!
Sweet, sweet home!
Sweet home, we shout again!

Ho, there! Bring out our nags!
No more our going lags,
We go; the threshold dear, to greet,
To fondly mothers' kisses meet:
We haste to all home-gladness sweet!

CHORUS.—Home, home, sweet home!
Home, home, sweet home!
Sweet, sweet home!
Sweet home, we shout again!

Pæans to our Penates raise!
They shall hear our voice of praise!
Why, with tardy-brightening rays,
Oh, sluggish-dawning Break-of-Day,
Didst thou our coming joys delay?

CHORUS.—Home, home, sweet home!
Home, home, sweet home!
Sweet, sweet home!
Sweet home, we shout again!

www.ingramcontent.com/pod-product-compliance
Lightning Source LLC
Chambersburg PA
CBHW021125020726
47500CB00003B/930